VALDOR: BIRTH OF THE IMPERIUM

*Order the full range of Horus Heresy novels, audio dramas
and audiobooks from blacklibrary.com*

THE HORUS HERESY®

VALDOR:
BIRTH OF THE IMPERIUM

CHRIS WRAIGHT

BLACK LIBRARY

A BLACK LIBRARY PUBLICATION

First published in 2019.
This edition published in Great Britain in 2023 by
Black Library, Games Workshop Ltd., Willow Road,
Nottingham, NG7 2WS, UK.

Represented by: Games Workshop Limited – Irish branch,
Unit 3, Lower Liffey Street, Dublin 1,
D01 K199, Ireland.

10 9 8 7 6 5 4 3 2 1

Produced by Games Workshop in Nottingham.
Cover illustration by Aaron Griffin.

See Black Library on the internet at

blacklibrary.com

Find out more about Games Workshop
and the worlds of Warhammer at

games-workshop.com

Printed and bound in the UK.

To Hannah, with love.

*With many thanks to Nick Kyme and to John French
for invaluable feedback and advice on the lore.*

THE HORUS HERESY®
It was a time of turmoil.

For thousands of years, Terra was divided,
its petty warlords vying for supremacy.

An Age of Strife reigned, and it was bloody.

Then came the Emperor…

Through His will and the armies of savage
Thunder Warriors did He bring order to a
chaotic world, His desire nothing less than the
preeminence of mankind.

Foremost amongst His soldiers were the
Custodian Guard, a peerless warrior brotherhood,
His generals and war leaders. The greatest of these
was Constantin Valdor, their dauntless captain.

Unity was inevitable, the tyrants crushed or
brought
to heel, alloyed under one banner.

And so the nascent Imperium was born.

A new era had begun.

As Old Night faded and the warp storms that had
estranged Terra from the distant tribes of humanity
abated, the Emperor's gaze turned to the mastery of
the stars themselves.

New armies were raised, stronger than the old:
the indomitable Space Marine Legions.

Unity had come, and so the Great Crusade
then beckoned…

Transcript
   Retrieved: *[Incognita]*
   Vector: *[Incognita]*
   Origin: Luna, transit station Aleph-Null-Null; prior, Imperial
Core audex general repository; prior, *[Incognita]*
   Determination: Uncertain; refer to senior adept
   Canister marker: Store; *Mundus est finem*
   Classification: *Occultis ad mortem*

   -- Begins (audex: Gothic antiqua A) --

   S1: Awake?
   S2: *[Qua nihil respondente.]*
   S1: *[Silentium.]* Please. Take your time.
   S2: Who…
   S1: Who are you?
   S2: *[Nihil respondente.]*

S1: You do not remember your name.

S2: No.

S1: Or where you came from.

S2: No.

S1: Would you tell me if you did?

S2: *[Silentium.]* I… do not know.

S1: You would. From this day, to the end of all days, you would tell me anything I asked of you, if you knew it.

S2: *[Silentium.]* Yes.

S1: So. What can I give you?

S2: *[Nihil respondente.]*

S1: Information. Data. In the days to come, that may be all I can give you. I can already feel it creeping up. You pay a price for all things, and this is mine – I will become less than human.

S2: Less than?

S1: And more. There was a saying, an old one – no such thing as a free lunch. *[Ridens.]* You make one bargain, become stronger. You make another, become weaker. It applies to mortals. It applies to gods. Not that I intend to become one.

S2: I do not– *[Intermissum.]*

S1: Forgive me. I have been alone a long time. I can talk, if allowed to. You need to know certain things, now.

S2: Yes.

S1: There is a grand bargain here.

S2: I understand it.

S1: Do you? Already? Good. Very good. What is the bargain?

S2: *[Silentium.]* Infinite power cannot be overcome. We are finite, limited by law. So, deception.

S1: Do you find that unworthy?

S2: No.

S1: Because it comes from me.

S2: Yes.

S1: Speak freely. For once, speak freely. You are only just awakened – there may be few chances left for you.

S2: *[Silentium.]* You will cheat them. You will cheat all of them. And us.

S1: A risky strategy.

S2: There are no others.

S1: You understand it. And, tell me – do you understand the full implication?

S2: Ruin. Total ruin.

S1: Good. And, now, tell me this – knowing all this, knowing the risks, the likely outcome, why did I make you?

S2: *[Silentium.]*

S1: Speak.

S2: *[Nihil respondente.]*

ONE

Sevuu watched the flyer come in from the west, low across the ravines of eastern Anatolya, a deepening sky at its back. He shaded his eyes with a dry palm, squinting against the glare of the slowly sinking sun. Before him stretched the baking stonescape of rock and smoulder, still angry, still hot.

The flyer trailed two lines of dirty smoke. As it neared, dipping in the heat, Sevuu noticed its chipped red hull, its old-style turbine nacelles. It was big – a twenty-seater, maybe – but out of shape.

Sevuu smiled. Just like her to find a rust-hulk, the kind of thing any out-of-luck merchant prince would scrape up from a salvage yard. He couldn't remember the last time he'd seen her in a Palace vehicle. All that gold didn't really suit her.

He waited, standing still as the dust billowed up around his robes. The flyer extended landing pads, and the turbines swivelled earthwards. In a whine-hail of engines, it came down, kicking up dry soil across the landing site.

Then he moved, walking gingerly across the rock-strewn field, covering his mouth against the grit with a mesh scarf. The first two people out of the flyer were her guards, chainmail armoured, environment masked, projectile-weapon clutching. Sevuu had never discovered what regiment or detachment she took her close protection from – it was hard, even now, to keep track of all the current, semi-current, legal and illegal military units on a world whose only real occupation for several mortal generations had been killing.

Then she emerged, waddling down the ramp, swaddled in grey skirts, clomping her heavy boots, eyes hidden behind thick shades. Her hair was tied up, wrapped around in a red scarf, exposing only patches of her dark, tough skin.

Sevuu went up to her, extending his hands in greeting. She grabbed them both, squeezing hard.

'Sevuu,' she said.

'Madam High Lord,' he replied.

'Ready to show me?'

'Everything,' he said.

On the journey, two things occurred to him as if for the first time, despite how often he had made the same flight and seen the same things.

The first was the vastness of the place. Soon after lifting again from the landing stage, locked down in the flyer's hold and pressed up against a smeary viewport, he could see the land wrinkle away towards the curved horizon, a mass of cranial defiles and pale orange mesas. The sky was still a pale blue in the west, darkening at the apex of the atmosphere's dome, and long shadows ran west-east.

This country had no settled name. It had been depopulated for hundreds of years, just another casualty of chem-clogged warfare and environmental collapse. So much of the globe was the same. Humanity had clung on during the years of strife, crammed within the iron shells of the great coastal cities that now peered across boiled-off seabeds, but not everywhere. For hundreds of kilometres, thousands of kilometres, there was nothing now – just the tick of poison-detectors and rad-counters, the scuttle of six-eyed rodents, the brush of a reproachful wind.

This place, he had been told, had once been called Urartu. There had been kings here, just as there had been kings everywhere – tech-warlords with violent courts, barely deserving the many titles they were given. So far, so unremarkable. You could have said the same about the wild steppes of Asia, the teeming weapon factories of Europa, the hyper-cities of Pan-Pacifica – all at one another's throats, gripped by the terror and ecstasy of killing.

But there *was* something about this place. Something primordial.

And that was the second thing. The rocks were old here. Very old. The ruins were old. The watercourses were old. You could smell the age, staining everything, humming softly under a surface cocktail of military-grade chemical spills.

Sevuu was not a historian. There had only been real historians operating on Terra for a short time, ever since He had brought them back into service, and so the past was to him as it was to almost everyone, a blurry mass of myth and conjecture. But you looked at the rocks, here. You ran your finger over them, and you felt where old rainfall had pattered and the hoof-prints of extinct animals were preserved, and you *knew*. You knew that a story had started here, so long ago that its opening words would never be remembered, but that the story itself still mattered, for it hadn't finished yet.

Sevuu looked over at High Lord Uwoma Kandawire, who was not looking through the viewport at the scenery. She was sitting in her chair, small and uncomfortable. Her hands gripped the armrests. She had taken her shades off, and that made it easier to see the unease on her face.

'You have already had a long journey,' Sevuu said.

Kandawire glanced up at him, roused from thoughts of her own, then shot him a wry smile.

'You'd have thought,' she said, 'that after all we've done, all we've gone through, we could design an atmospheric flyer that didn't make me puke.'

Sevuu nodded. Of course, the High Lord was incorrect. There were plenty of flyers that she could have taken, ones that glided through the air with nary a vibration, air-conditioned and whisper-quiet; but they were ostentatious and expensive and would have been noticed by any of the hundreds of make-shift intelligence operations working both within and without the Palace system. And so she, Mistress of the Lex Pacifica and commander of a bureaucracy of thousands, had made herself pukesome on a rattling hunk of poorly riveted steel. Admirable devotion to the cause.

'Not far now,' Sevuu said.

Kandawire pushed her shoulders back, hard into the flaking synthleather padding, and tried to ride the judder. 'I read your 'slate bulletin,' she said. 'Anything to add before we arrive?'

Sevuu shook his head. 'Not really. I can't decide if they were careless, or we were thorough.'

'You were thorough. It's why I chose you.'

'Or they thought, with some justification, that no one cared enough to look.'

'Yes, yes,' she said. 'That too.' For the first time, she looked out of her viewport, where the sky was falling away into that deep, oceanic blue that ushered in sunset. Stars were already visible in the east, tiny points of light purer than any now gen-erated on a spoiled world. 'I'm grateful to you, that you took this on. I'm mindful of the dangers you all faced.'

Sevuu bowed, appreciative. 'It has been fascinating.'

'I feel, to be honest, that I already have much of what I need. Your report was as complete as ever. But I–'

'–needed to see for yourself.'

Kandawire smiled. 'We do, don't we?' She turned away from the viewport. 'Even now, that hasn't changed.'

A light blinked on the overhead panel, and the flyer began to dip into its descent. The vibration became worse.

'Would anything change your mind?' Sevuu asked.

'Plenty,' Kandawire said. 'I want to be wrong. I always have.'

The shaking hit a rhythmic stride, marking their descent down to another dirt-blown landing strip bordering what had once, on the edge of a species' memory, deserved the name civilisation.

'You're not often wrong,' said Sevuu.

They did not ascend the mountain that day.

By the time they'd come down to the final-stage landing ground, the compound's security lumens were at full beam and the sun was burning its way into a distant, still war-ravaged, west. Sevuu escorted Kandawire through the streets of his temporary township – a dirty grid of prefab accommodation blocks on the edge of the landing strip, airlifted in two months ago and bolted together against the elements. The wind was blowing from the high eastern scarps, stirring the dust into spirals. Sevuu had donned an environment mask by then, but Kandawire seemed content to wrap her scarf around her face and huddle against the gritty breeze.

The security detail that met them was from Sevuu's command – twelve troopers of the Yoyoda Servine 12th, drawn from a regiment that had seen active service nine months ago half-way across the planet and had since been put on less arduous duty to recover. They were good, professional men and women, but Kandawire's bodyguards looked altogether more threatening as they fanned out across the landing site.

Sevuu took the High Lord to her quarters – one of the larger units, cleared hurriedly and kitted out with a working heater-unit. She took a single look at it and hid her dismay reasonably well. Then he bade her a good night, closed the doors and double-checked the security details.

He didn't sleep much after that. His own quarters were draughty, and once the sun disappeared the temperature plummeted. He reviewed his work. He tried to ignore the clump and bang of armed troops patrolling the perimeter fence. Eventually, he lay on his sagging cot, staring at the ceiling, thinking back over the past weeks of toil and what it all meant, or didn't mean. Gradually, slinking around the edges of his blinds, sunlight crept back in, and another day had passed.

Sighing, he got to his feet, washed at the basin, tried to make his crumpled uniform look a little less disgraceful. A shot of recaff and a carb-stick later and he was making his way back to Kandawire's unit. He knocked on the door. When she opened it, she looked crisp and businesslike, freshly draped in those long robes she always wore, the scarf artfully arranged again – a sky-blue one, this time.

'Sleep?' he asked.

'Better than you, by the looks of things,' said Kandawire, gingerly stepping down the metal steps.

They met their escort – more of the chainmail-armoured soldiers – and took a convoy of six trucks out of the eastern gate and up into the highlands beyond. Five of the carriers were Odion troop haulers, heavy and bolstered with thick metal plating. Theirs was a civilian transport, adapted for the rough terrain and, as a result, boneshakingly uncomfortable.

The air was crisp and clear, still cold although warming fast. The rockscape stretched away from them in all directions, bare and glistening with the last of the dew. It was a pale brown, like flesh. Ahead loomed their destination.

'Impressive,' said Kandawire, tilting her shades down and peering over the rim. 'A suitable location for the drama of it, at least.'

It was a long trek up the dirt tracks, ones that were barely used by any but the old smuggler-gang remnants. Scrub clung to the margins, black-leaved and sparse. You could still taste the rads here, making the air pungent like spilled spice.

Ahead of them, it loomed – double-peaked, a sweep of mountain like a white wave. Behind its shoulders marched the badlands of the lesser Caucasus, snow-capped and wind-blasted, but ahead of its skirts there was nothing but more emptiness.

The mountain. Ararat. Storied since the earliest days of humanity, a name recorded and erased and recorded again in a thousand holy palimpsests, all of them now proscribed and destined for the incinerators.

'There's nothing here,' Sevuu said, bracing himself against the movement of the transport. 'Nothing left to fight over. I still don't understand it.'

'There's plenty here,' said Kandawire. 'On the other side of this range, a few hundred kilometres away, there's an empire. One responsible for the death of a whole army. We sent it in, it never came out.'

Sevuu looked at her, startled. 'Really?' he asked.

'Even now.' Kandawire looked like she was enjoying herself. 'Its days are marked, of course. All these places – their days are marked. We'll send another army in there, one day. It's all about choosing the moment.'

'So this was a warning, here,' Sevuu said, cautiously. 'A display of strength.'

'I don't think so. I think the symbolism was more important.' Kandawire rubbed her elbows to get the blood moving.

The bumps and rocking were getting arduous. 'But, in a way, it's always been about strength, this whole thing, from beginning to end. The question we should be asking is – what kind?'

'And you have an answer to that.'

'I have an answer to everything,' said Kandawire. 'The right one, I hope.'

'No doubt.'

Now they were climbing higher, riding the switchbacked trails over deep defiles. It got hotter inside the transports as the sun climbed with them, boiling off the last of the mists and making the air shimmer. The atmosphere became thin, making the engines labour. It took several hours of shaking and revving across the uneven terrain before, finally, the narrow, embedded shaft of Sevuu's locator-spear came into view. The transports shuddered to a halt, steaming in the sun's glare. One by one, the guards disembarked, looking around themselves warily.

Sevuu dropped to the ground and offered Kandawire a hand. Then they walked, their limbs stiff, past the metre-high locator-spear and out across the massif beyond.

Flags snapped everywhere, caught in the strong breeze. Long trenches had been dug across the landscape, two metres deep and already scudded with snow. Workers huddled against the biting breeze, some of them with thin strips of exposed flesh under environment wrappers, others with dumb augmetics glinting. They went slowly, both human and servitor, half from the cold, half from the need to pay close attention to what they were doing.

Kandawire surveyed the scene, all the while clambering over the frost-glistening gravel. Sevuu came with her, poised to offer an arm, should she need one. The cold air was already making his throat ache.

'A suitable site,' she said, looking back and forth, up to the cliffs above, down to the long snaking road that had brought them here. 'I'm not a soldier, you understand.'

'I understand,' said Sevuu.

She smiled at him – a flash of white teeth. 'I can see why they did it here, though. Hemmed in, very high up. Flyers would struggle, yes? But a wide place where an army – where two armies – could meet. A proper contest.' She breathed in, deeply. She put her hands on her hips, and stopped moving. 'This is where it happened, then.'

Sevuu kept walking. 'I wanted to show you this one.'

They picked their way between trenches, watched all the way by their chaperones. Kandawire started to pant – this was not her natural element – and her chainmail escorts moved in closer in case she needed them.

Soon the trenches fell away behind them, one by one, filled with their gravel-dusted items. The soft chitter of servitor-binaric faded, and they were standing on the margins, where the plain began to break up into fractured rock shelves. A few hundred metres further, and the land plummeted again, falling away in cloud-wreathed steps.

Sevuu squatted down beside the flapping skirts of a pinned awning, pushing his visor back as he did so. Kandawire joined him, and he caught a faint whiff of perfume – an urban scent, one worn in the growing cities of the south-east, not something to take into the wastes.

He lifted the protective plastek sheets carefully, seeing how the dew clung to the earth under them. The objects revealed were small – just fragments of wholes, shrapnel and jetsam. He reached for one of them, picking it up carefully and turning it over in his palm.

'We get a lot of these,' he said, handing it to Kandawire.

She took it, holding it up to the light. 'Raptor Imperialis,' she said, narrowing her eyes. Her fingers rubbed grit from the lacquer, revealing an armour-pin and its device – an eagle's head surrounded by four thin jags of lightning. The image held her gaze for a long time. 'I argued against this image,' she said, thoughtfully. 'I told them it set the wrong tone. We were builders, not destroyers. An eagle builds nothing but its own eyrie, and a storm merely ravages. One of many arguments I lost. They were after a different message.'

'The armour pieces are mixed. Some analyse as a ceramic compound, something very strong, heat-resistant, nothing I've seen before. Other pieces are metal – steel, even iron. And then there's the rarest of all. We can't even get it through the analysers without them breaking. To the touch, some of the fragments are still warm. And they look for all the world like–'

'Gold,' said Kandawire, getting back to her feet. She stowed the armour-fragment away. 'Gold that never tarnishes, gold to withstand every flame. It's not really gold, though. It just looks like it.'

'I have a lot more to show you,' Sevuu said.

'How many died?'

He paused. 'Thousands. Tens of thousands. More than we can count here.'

Kandawire nodded. Her fingers, wrapped in linen, curled up. 'You won't need to. I want you gone in two days. I want all this taken down and the compound pulled up.'

'But we haven't–'

'It's dangerous. It's right what they say – the truth is in the earth.' She started to walk again, a limping gait that betrayed her lack of conditioning. 'I've seen all I need to.'

'Like I said. I have no idea *why*,' Sevuu said, watching her go. 'You read the report. It looks… senseless.'

Kandawire kept on going.

'It wasn't,' she said, picking her way through the half-frozen detritus of war. 'And it's not the end.'

TWO

It was a ludicrous place for a city.

The air was painfully thin, even with the embedded processors clattering along at full tilt, squirting oxygen into an altitude never designed for human lungs. It had taken years to stabilise the climate here, and continual effort was still required to maintain what had been painfully won. If the processors ever failed, or if the nuclear power plants buried deep in the mountains' roots ever faltered, this place would revert to what it had been for most of its long history – a silent waste at the roof of the world, marked by nothing but hard-packed snow and naked rock.

Few observers ever speculated why such a location had been chosen for the site of the new capital. Few ever speculated on any of His actions, these days – it had become commonplace to simply accept them. There had to be a reason, or He would not have done it. The recent decades of spectacular success had made people think He was invincible, inerrant, omnipotent.

Dangerous thoughts. They ran counter to the very heart's-blood of the whole enterprise, but once they were formulated, they were so particularly, so irritatingly, hard to stamp out.

So there were organisations dedicated to eradicating difficult ideas. They operated subtly, for the most part – enforcing literature bans, having quiet words with the right, or the wrong, people – but Terra was still a violent world, still in the birth pangs of its new future, and there were times when sharper tools were needed. Some observers maintained that the planet was all but united now, and that only sporadic actions were necessary to keep a lid on the worst of long-engrained human nature. 'Compliance' actions, they called them. None of this, sadly, was true. Old powers still cultivated support in the dark soils of rad-infested valleys. Some were deluded, unable to accept the new truth of a dawning age. Others knew just what was happening, and fought to prevent its sunrise.

Even so, the idea was the most dangerous part. The notion, the belief – *belief*, that most lingering of the old pathologies, clinging with withered fingertips on to the edge of the long fall into oblivion.

'I teach the end of belief,' He had said, once, so it was written. 'I am its terminus, its replacement. After me, there will only be perception, a sight of the single truth, glimpsed from distance.'

The Custodian Samonas had no belief, at least not in the sense of something superstitious, something grasping at the numinous. If he had once, as a child, been able to entertain such phantasms, that capability had been scrubbed out of him a long time ago. He did not miss it. Samonas had no regrets. Regrets were for the mass of humanity, the herds he had been appointed to watch over. For one of his order, there were only the stark binaries left: to know, to be ignorant; to overcome, to be defeated; to be loyal, to be traitor.

So when he looked out over the Palace – as he knew, one

day, it would routinely be called – he did not share in the fantastical idea that the half-finished domes and spires had been somehow fated to be raised here, or that its existence was proof of some ineffable divine will, for it was merely *there*. The order had been given. Now his purpose was to safeguard it, just as his purpose had always been to safeguard the Creations.

He entertained a residual interest in the progress of the techwrights. He had watched the Tower of Hegemon rise, slowly, from extravagantly solid foundations. To the north, across a deep valley slowly filling with rockcrete piers, he had seen the great halls of the Senatorum Imperialis take shape. The size had impressed him – a typically bold statement of vision. For centuries, Terra had been a world of mediocre warlords' roosts, crumbling palaces, ruins that slowly subsided into dust-drifts. This was something else.

'I do not truly see the need for it,' Kallander, the first chancellor, had once confided, irritably. As the man responsible for finding the coin necessary for its construction, he could be forgiven for doubting the purpose of it all.

Samonas understood, though. He understood that, once complete, this fortress would daunt the mortal soul. Once complete, it would project such an air of domination that no enemy would ever contemplate attacking it, unless they had been driven into some kind of bestial madness and no longer feared total annihilation.

He had seen the plans for the rest, too. He had seen blueprints for constructions of totally unknown purpose. Some of these would be immensely tall, just like the chamber of the Senatorum. Other galleries went down a long way. Despite the punishing environment, the Palace was not the first great fortress to be made here. As ever on Terra, foundations had been laid upon foundations. Who knew where the trail eventually ended? Perhaps even He did not. Samonas did not know how long He had been alive for, and what He had seen across those many years.

That was natural. The Emperor, as they all called Him, was bounded by limitation. He required servants. He required allies, and He required tools. Some of these tools were trivial and plentiful, like the workers of the Masonic guilds who painstakingly engraved the stone capitals atop their skyscrapers of scaffolding. Some were rare and potent, like Samonas himself. Some were powerful almost beyond conception – creations of such outsized, bafflingly outrageous capability that one was tempted to echo Kallander's scepticism, and fail to 'see the need'.

The greatest of these creatures was back in the Palace, now, withdrawn from the wars in the west, where the Emperor and His Regent still remained, so the reports went. He had been pulled from the fighting. That would not make his mood a cheerful one.

So Samonas walked a little faster than he would normally have done. His boots, exquisite creations unique to him, clinked on the glass-marble with a fractionally more intense rhythm, not that any mortal ears would have detected the difference. By the time he had arrived at his destination, his total expenditure of energy was close to a single percentage point higher than the baseline estimate for such a short journey.

Perhaps he could have done better. Then again, that was always the assessment.

'Come.'

The voice came from the other side of the heavy oak doors. It was as familiar to Samonas as his own – a sonorous voice, preternaturally calm, effortlessly confident, slighter than you'd expect, as translucent, in its own way, as the unbroken snow-palls outside. It was the voice of command. It was the voice of order. It was the voice of infinite violence, held back – barely – within a shell of fragile artifice.

He went in.

'Captain-general,' Samonas said, bowing.

Captain-general. A nondescript term for an office of colossal power. In the early days, all their titles had been modest, and it had only been the rapid expansion of the scholar class that had brought about the absurdities of Gothic rank inflation. Then again, this one had seen it all. He had been there from before the beginning, they said: the first of the Order, coeval with the Sigillite, the final element of the trinity that had brought a world to heel.

Emperor, Sorcerer, Warrior.

He was standing, looking out of a wide crystalflex window at the peaks in the west. His tall frame – far taller than the tallest unaltered human, a cathedral of hard-edged muscle and bone – made the room's fittings shrink. He wore a pale robe, fine-spun, lined with gold. His head was bare, exposing a master-crafted ring of thread-implants around his neck. He stood with a dancer's bearing, the unconscious poise that all of the Order shared, ready, at the prompt of a thought, to mobilise all that spectacular gene magick and biomancy into a whirl of destructive action, but for now still, held together, dormant.

He turned, exposing his face. It was lean, a soft collection of taut lines.

'I can imagine it now,' Constantin Valdor said. 'As it will be, when complete. I never could, before.'

Samonas nodded. The grand plan was becoming increasingly obvious as the walls and the towers began to climb their way into the frosty airs. 'A masterful vision,' he ventured.

'You think so?' Valdor regarded him coolly. Valdor regarded most things coolly. 'A ludicrous place for a city. I told Him that myself.'

'It will be a symbol.'

'We are the symbols.'

So his master's humours were cold, just as predicted. It was unlikely Valdor truly intended criticism of the Emperor. It was unlikely that Valdor, or Samonas, or any of the Order, were truly capable of sustained criticism of Him.

We are extensions of a single will, Samonas had been told, on awakening from the final trial, decades ago. *We are adjuncts, we are orbitals. We are the periphery of the immortal, not its heart.*

'Will He return soon?' Samonas ventured.

'No.' Valdor turned back to the mountains. 'At least that will give the techwrights time to finish it.'

'I have reports, if you wish to read them.'

Valdor turned back towards him, and there was the spectre of a half-smile, briefly. 'Diligent Samonas,' he said. 'Tell me of her.'

Samonas hesitated. Some matters were delicate, hard to handle even for one of his training. 'She is near, now,' he said. 'Closing on her objective. I completed my researches, and the threat is significant. If you were asking for counsel–'

'I was not. But give me it, since you've started.'

'End her now.'

Valdor thought on that for a moment. 'She is that dangerous?'

'She knows.'

'Knowledge is no crime.'

'In itself, no. But what is done with it, that can be.'

Valdor moved away from the window. 'No. Not yet.' He drew in a breath, then winced a little. The air was antiseptic here, still raw from the cyclers, and was no substitute for the real thing. 'This is a new age, *vestarios*. An age of law. I will not succumb to a warlord's urges, and nor should you.'

'It is understood, captain-general.'

'Gather evidence. Find a weakness, a slip in resolve.'

'It is understood, captain-general.'

'Is she here?'

'Yes.'

'Then this should be trivial, for one of your talents.'

Samonas looked up, briefly entertaining the idea he was being mocked. Nothing was trivial, not in this place. 'She has His trust.'

Valdor did not smile. 'I do not think He *trusts*, Samonas. Even we can trust, in an idea, or an order, but He has nothing. Be mindful – the stronger you become, the weaker everything around you is. He can grasp on to nothing, for His grip will break it. Imagine that. Imagine the solitude of it.'

He turned away. His mood seemed capricious, or maybe the weariness was telling, even for one of his near-infinite resources. Samonas said nothing, waiting for it to play out.

'I would not welcome seeing her ended,' he said, at length. 'She is a symbol too, of a kind. A better kind than we are, maybe.'

'I will bear that in mind,' said Samonas.

'But if the moment comes, of course.'

'Your sanction, captain-general?'

'You will use your judgement.'

And that was the end of it. Samonas bowed again, and withdrew, retracing his steps back to the heavy doors. By the time he pulled them closed, Valdor was facing back out into the landscape beyond, hands clasped behind his back.

He looked as solid as the peaks beyond, or more so, as if he would outlast them, and still be standing there when they were no more than rubble, just there, in that place, against the crystal screen where the air was thin.

But then many things had looked eternal, at the start. That was the great lesson of Unification – none of it was. Nothing but Him, and He was not here yet, and so all could yet be doubted.

So Samonas closed the doors. There was work to do.

THREE

It was a fantastic place for a city – high up, away from the rads and the filth, one of the few places that had never been despoiled, still hard and clear and unsullied.

Kandawire didn't approve of everything that had been done over the last fifty years of debate and disagreement, but building the seat of Unity here was evidently the correct decision. All still living on Terra looked up to this place. No warlord had ever conquered it. The masses would lift their heads from their seamy plains and swamps, turn away from the degraded hive-sumps and sprawl-cities, and see something untrammelled rise into impossible heights, clean and unmatchable, a signal to the future.

One day, of course. For now, it was a building site, the largest ever marshalled by human hands, toiling against the punishing elements to raise an icon of defiance. It was cold, the mud was frozen. The lumens would blink out at a moment's notice. The piped water was gritty, and seldom got hot even when the generator-banks were working.

That last one was an irritant. After the long atmospheric stage to Himalazia, it would have been good to relax in a pulse-shower, washing the dust from her body, but instead it had been a matter of grimly bearing the ice-cold spears of water before they guttered out in a splurt of muck. The torrent of expletives from her chambers had been enough to send order-lies scurrying, but there was little they could do when the whole complex was still half-finished. She emerged in a foul state, her hair disarranged and sodden, all fatigue dispelled by fury.

She stomped into the antechamber, where her aide-de-camp, Armina, was wrestling with a pile of comm-tubes freshly des-patched by a messenger drone.

'I'm running late,' Kandawire announced.

Armina looked up at her, brushing away a strand of hair.

Kandawire was as black as jet, Armina was as white as chalk. Kandawire's hair was wiry and unruly, Armina's was straw-pale and flat. The two of them were like the termini of a spectrum illustration – the full range of humanity, its vigorous extremes, still popping up after tangled millennia of mingled breeding.

'He will expect you to be on time,' Armina said, sniffing in disapproval.

Kandawire went over to a sideboard and reached for a jewellery casket. 'You have no appreciation for *status*, Armina,' she said. 'What signal would it send, if I turned up in the slot he'd offered me?' She picked out a silver necklace, studded with tiny pearls, lifting it up to the light. 'I'm a bloody High Lord. I turn up when I want to.'

Armina shook her head. 'You could wear it a little more lightly.'

Kandawire turned, holding the necklace up to her throat. 'Really? I like it.'

'Your *office*.' Armina went back to sorting the comm-tubes, extracting the ciphered innards and placing them in the correct order into the speaker-coils. 'This bravado fools only fools. He'd only have to flick his fingers,' Armina snapped her own, 'and that would be your neck, gone.'

'He'd not dare,' said Kandawire, unclasping the chain and donning it. 'There's more than one kind of strength, something I keep telling you.'

'Over and over,' Armina mumbled.

'The law binds them,' Kandawire went on. 'That's what makes this Emperor worth serving.' The clasp clicked closed, and she let her hands fall again. 'At least, that is what we must believe.'

'Will you at least make the attempt not to insult him?'

Kandawire tilted a mirror and adjusted her scarf and wrapped dress. 'He is a Custodian. They are, so I have always been led to believe, impervious to insults. We are like gnats to them. Less than gnats – our bites don't penetrate their skin.'

Armina put the last tube into the last coil. 'There is much to do here,' she said, chidingly. 'You have been away for a long time already, working on… whatever it is. You have responsibilities, High Lord.'

Kandawire came up to her, took both her hands in her own. 'I know. That is why I do this. Keep putting things in order for me.'

Armina smiled. 'So you can disarrange them again.'

'That's my job.'

Armina pulled her hands away, and returned to the coils. Her fingers danced over the controls, and sigils began to pulse into the decoders. 'At least, then, be careful,' she said.

'Ensure you retain contact with Ophar,' said Kandawire, walking towards the great doors. 'If you wish to worry about anyone, worry about him. I, on the other hand, as always, will be fine.'

That was not strictly accurate. For most of her life, Uwoma Kandawire had been very far from fine. It had been a vanishingly rare thing, on Terra, for anyone at all to be *fine*. In close and living memory, the entire planet had been a gangster-riddled rock, squabbled over only by the amoral and the debauched. Every part of it had been backward and dangerous, and staying alive had been a matter of luck, or maybe deviousness, or maybe, just now and then, judgement.

She had been born into a relatively wealthy family within what had then been the Banda Confederacy in the extreme south-eastern corner of Afrik. Modest wealth allowed them certain privileges – security guards around the edge of their compound, a degree of regularity in food supply, access to what few trappings of civilisation still clung on along the baked-dry coastal belt.

She still remembered, as a young girl, sitting on the deserted beach in the evening, the sand dirty, the desiccated old ocean-bowl just a few metres from her gritty bare feet. Flickers of distant lightning had been dancing along an infinite horizon. Those living nearby had called the ocean, while it had existed, *zothasa* – endless, as if it never found another shore.

Kandawire knew better. There were a few vid-books in her mother's library, and one of those contained an atlas. The lith-cast unit had broken a long time ago, but you could still shine a torch through the aperture and project the blurred trace of the coastlines onto a whitewashed wall. Once she'd learned that trick, she'd spent hours marking them out, trying to read the tiny labels and wondering what kinds of people lived in those places that she would never be able to visit. She imagined them all, naturally, as being much like her. Maybe many of them were wise and cultivated, living in cities lined with orange groves and water fountains. Or maybe most were like the *zooipa*, the savages of the north with their red-painted trucks and flame-bringers, who lived in hovels, ate human flesh for sustenance and raided for what little else they wanted.

She remembered sitting by the thin bars of the electro-heater in the evenings, her dress itchy from the dust, as her father traced his own bony finger along the burned-stick marks she had made on the wall.

'You could once travel from here to here,' he had said, jabbing at islands and inlets running up the eastern seaboard. 'There were cities this far up, once. Huge, huge places, built on concrete platforms, out into the sea. They sucked the water up, like you suck goat's milk through a straw, and scrubbed the salt from it. That was the only way they could keep the people from dying of thirst.'

'What do they do now?' she had asked, wide-eyed, chewing on her fingernails.

'I do not know,' her father had said. 'Nothing works much, any more. Perhaps the zooipa raided there, like they did everywhere else. I expect those cities are empty, now.'

That had made her angry. All such stories had made her angry. '*Why* does nothing work any more?' she had demanded.

She still remembered her father's stubbly chin, his face that was skinny from not getting enough to eat, and those sad, intelligent eyes. 'Because the warrior is in charge, *kondedwa*. Whenever the warrior is in charge, things stop working. For things to work, the warrior is the servant of the worker. You see it? The worker makes things work.'

'The warrior makes...'

'Wars.'

But the warriors were the only ones who made anything, back then. They were the only ones with the weapons, with the coin, with the energy. Nothing could stand in their way for long – when the mood came upon them, as it did often, they would ravage down the long, dry coast, burning and breaking. The sand would darken with blood for a few days, and the red earth would grow sticky with engine oil, and no one would sit under the shadow of the splintered palms and gaze out over the empty sea.

Now, when Kandawire thought back, she wondered that she had survived at all. Her mother had not, dying of the cancer that was now easily treatable in major Imperial cities – a result, Kandawire found out later, of the radiation-laced munitions still lurking in the grit of her homeland. Her father did not either; the raids eventually reached far enough south to swallow up the family compound, just as they had done to so many others, snuffing out the few bright points of sanctuary along that desolate littoral.

It had been Ophar who had rescued her. Ophar, with his spindly limbs and bulging eyes. Ophar looked like a child's rag-toy, which was why no one took him seriously. He had pulled her from her cot and tried to huddle her out to the last of the land-transports before the zooipa broke through the perimeter. Precocious as ever, she had not let him drag her to safety, but had stamped her feet and refused to go until he had rescued the vid-book projector too.

She had not gone back for her father. She had not gone back for any of the staff who had nursed and entertained her. Back then, with a spoiled child's sense of self-importance, she had wanted the one thing that made her happy, that allowed her to dream of other worlds and other places.

Kandawire still winced at the memory. It had haunted her ever since, spiking at her conscience. She could have done nothing much to help, in all honesty, but still it rankled that she had never tried. All she had left now were those memories, those injunctions.

The worker makes things work.

Now, in the high airs above the Palace's central zone within her luxurious air-car, Kandawire looked over at the pilot of the flyer, with her starched collar and trim epaulettes. She glanced at the guards on either side of her, a man and a woman, both in the heavy chainmail armour that gave her that elusive sense of physical security. They performed their duties with a quiet attention to detail that reflected well, not only on them, but on the system that had created them. Kandawire could raise her pudgy, ring-encrusted finger, and they would follow any order she gave them.

The warrior is the servant of the worker.

So fragile, that arrangement. So easy to pull apart.

'Bring us down on the minor platform, please,' Kandawire said.

The pilot nodded, and the air-car dipped into a controlled descent. Ahead of them, the skeleton of Third Proscribed Area, known by anyone with any decent information as the Tower of Hegemon, filled the forward viewscreens. It looked like some heavy outer shielding was being lifted into position, obscuring a thick core of rockcrete piles. The topmost pinnacle was like a finger flayed of its flesh, a needle of bone against the white sky.

They docked at the lesser of the two air-platforms, to be greeted by a welcome party of Tower serfs. As ever, they were polite, soft-spoken, with eyes that seemed to see right through you. The passage to the captain-general's private chambers was efficient and quick, laced with expert small talk. The one who accompanied her, a slim woman with amber-brown skin called Callix, had the polished air of an aristocrat, or perhaps an academic, or maybe an archaeologist. She asked courteous questions, gave semi-contentful answers and smiled coolly the whole time.

It was so hard not to hate those people.

Soon they were all gone, along with Kandawire's bodyguards, leaving her alone in a marble-floored chamber of white stone walls. Late afternoon sun filtered in through narrow windows, designed to look like enlarged arrow-slits. The architecture was monolithic, like some fortress or castle from the forgotten past. There were no pictures, no ornaments, no fountains or decorative plants. The entire space was cold, pale, flat and unreflective.

Set in the heart of the floor, before the largest set of windows, were two seats facing one another. The one on the left was of human dimensions, and stood empty. The one on the right was twice the size, and was occupied.

'Sit, please,' its owner said, gesturing to the empty space.

Before she knew what she was doing, Kandawire found herself complying. Then she looked up, and faced, for the first time ever at such close range, the object of her enquiries: Valdor, the Emperor's Spear.

It was impossible, even for her, not to feel a spike of fear. It was impossible not to sense the cold sweat rising, the fight-or-flight mechanism kick in, the desire to look away, to reach for something to defend herself with.

With effort, she met his gaze.

'A good journey?' he asked.

It would have been nice to have replied with something clever, or defiant – something fitting her high station. In the event, she found her mouth had gone strangely dry.

'Yes,' was all she could get out.

At least, though, it was begun now. She had been told it would never happen, that he would never agree, and that it would be a waste of her time, since nothing could be discovered from this source that he did not wish to be discovered.

They had all been wrong about the first of those. Hopefully they would be wrong about the rest, too.

She took a breath.

'Constantin Valdor, captain-general of the Legio Custodes,' she said, trying to keep her voice level. 'By the authority vested in me by the High Council of Terra, I hereby place you under a state of formal enquiry. By statute of the Lex Pacifica, you are required to answer all and any of my questions. An audex transcript will be made available in due course. Do you have any queries, before we begin?'

He was so like the rest of them – so calm, so icily assured. She wondered then if anything, ever, had given him a reason to break a sweat, or to lose that magisterial air of total command. This was a farce. He could end it at any time, and there was nothing she could do. She wondered, her heart thudding, if Armina was right, and this whole charade was little more than a signature over her death warrant.

But she had to keep going, now. It had been started, and must now be finished.

'None at all, High Lord,' Valdor said, placing his hands lightly on his lap. 'I suggest we commence. So, what do you wish to know?'

FOUR

Ophar was uncomfortable in his uniform. He was uncomfortable in most uniforms, and most clothes, and had come to accept that his physical dimensions meant that he probably always would be.

He had been gangly since birth, possessed of limbs that constantly seemed to be trying to make their own way in the world. Now he was old, too. He was older than he'd ever expected to be, his life extended by the treatments available in this terrifying, exciting new world of possibility. He didn't even know exactly how old he was, since the earliest years in the Banda settlements had been chaotic and violent, but he knew that, had he not left when he did, he would not still be irritably reflecting on ill-fitting clothes, or on anything at all.

Occasionally he would ponder this strange turn of events, when his duties allowed him. He could still experience a powerful sense of shock at the pace at which everything had changed. Sometimes, but not often, he would miss the old world, with his cogitated plan-overlays had recalculated. It had been a precious moment, one in which he picked up a good slug of data to be analysed later.

He saw them, up on the ramparts, heading away, one by one. Golden warriors, plumed with crimson, just tiny dots in the distance and part-hazed by the dust in the air. They were already the symbols of the place, its guardians, the 'custodians', not just of the Palace, but the Imperium itself. No one knew how many there were, not even Uwoma. That was for him to find out, of course, though the results were already beginning to surprise him.

That had been two nights ago. Now he was on the trail of different quarry, one of considerably less elevated pedigree but no less importance, at least to the matter at hand.

Night was falling, though the murmur and clank of construction never ceased. As the light died in the west, the lumens flickered on, spilling weak orange light across the gritty thoroughfares. Ophar descended through the outer tangle of the Masonic quarters, where the hab-blocks were rammed up tight and the shadows in the narrow streets lay heavy.

It was a bustling, claustrophobic space, every inch of it crushed with the steady movement of people. Neon signs had been slung overhead, some proclaiming gaudy Imperial propaganda – *A New Age Dawns. The Emperor Delivers It! Report All Suspicious Activity To Your Local Arbites Tower* – others with commercials from the big trading guilds. Out of the mountain wind, the smells became more varied – medical supplies with their chemical tang, caged animals smuggled in under the noses of the customs watchers, the earthy stinks of close-packed humanity. Music blared from cheap voxcasters, tinny electrosynth ballads, stirring military anthems sung by regimental choirs, all blending into a cacophony that swilled and swirled through the narrow passages and made the hubbub of different dialects all the more unintelligible.

He was not the only robed official making his way through the jostling masses, and few gave him a second glance. Everything had an air of impermanence, of semi-completion, as if foundations were still being settled into place and no one quite knew just what would be piled on top of them yet.

He stepped aside to allow the passage of a big, lurching personnel carrier, then slipped down a narrow side street. In the distance, he could just make out the towering watch-piers of the checkpoint gate, several storeys higher than the surrounding buildings. That was where most of the incoming traffic from the southern approach highways came in, and he knew there were queues of transports stretching far out into the landscape beyond, waiting for their turn for scrutiny. Several flyers hung like hawks in the evening gloaming, their autoguns trained to respond to the first sign of disturbance. This was a weak point, a point of danger, a point of opportunity. All gates were.

Away from the main thoroughfare, things got darker and quieter. He passed open doorways with occupants backlit by grimy lumens – families crammed into one-room apartments, children squalling, arguments floating out into the night air. He found the stairwell and dropped down a tight spiral of metal steps. The smell of some oily cooking wafted up from grilles in the brick walls on either side, and soon he was before a blastplate-door with a slit opening. He bent down and rapped on it – three knocks, then two more.

A panel flashed up with a red sigil-stream, a meaningless collection of runes unless you knew what to look for. Ophar inserted the lockword into the slot, and waited for the clunk. He pressed his face up against a glassy panel by the door hinges, and felt the hot prickle of a dermal scan. Then the locks snapped, and the door swung inwards.

After that, there were more stairs, going down again, getting hotter and darker. He was frisked by a burly guard who looked

Kandawire found herself strangely reluctant to begin, now that the moment had come. It was as if, having come so far, reaching the end was something to be swerved away from.

She gestured to the disc, and it pulsed into a soft standby light.

'I would like to begin with Maulland Sen,' she said.

'Maulland Sen,' Valdor replied. 'That is not a name I recall with any fondness.'

FIVE

Maulland Sen. That is not a name I recall with any fondness. Few remember it now at all, outside the Order.

[How many years ago?]

One hundred and twenty-six. More than a mortal lifetime.

[Not something that affects you, I suppose.]

Not in the same way. It was a confederacy of states. They had banded together during the worst years of anarchy. The climate is severe in those latitudes – that was also a factor. In those days, the weather satellites were all destroyed, and the winters had become punishing. Some form of association would have been required to avoid substantive depopulation, just as in other areas of the globe where the structures of civilisation had degraded beyond recall.

I remember the rock. It was black, like oil. The skies were heavy, and there were storms every day of the campaign, as if the heavens themselves were set against us. Equipment froze before we could use it. At every dawn we would have to light fires under the engines of the transports before we could use them. And the wind. It was like a scream, never ceasing.

[Tell me of the campaign orders. The preliminaries.]

This was in the early years of active expansion. The Emperor's plans had been in progress for decades by then, but we had not shown our hand openly in many places. Our stated territorial holdings were modest – enough to guarantee access to the materials we needed, and to impose a cordon around the sites where our researches needed to be protected. Only when these were fully secured and our forces mustered in numbers could we advance without the stealth we had previously employed.

Maulland Sen was not the first kingdom we conquered – it was too far from our established centres of control. However, I believe He had marked it out for particular attention from the start. In a world of abominations, it nevertheless stood out. We had heard all the stories and had studied the spies' reports. And He knew the place. He had been there before.

[For the transcript, by 'He', you mean–]

The Emperor. Of course. He was fully aware of the practices conducted there and wished to eradicate them as soon as He had the power to. That was always the principal objective, you understand, even in those early years. We were not simply fighting for territory – we were fighting to remove the taint of sorcery from Terra. I see your smile. Again, this is now not widely understood. A consequence of our success, I suppose. Say 'sorcery' now, and you will provoke a laugh of disbelief, but during the anarchy, all manner of beliefs were held, which led many into moral corruption. The human soul, if left untended, tends to moral corruption, and that opens doors. This world had been left untended for a very long time. Many doors had been left open.

Maulland Sen was a kingdom of witches at the roof of the

world. A realm closer to a nightmare would be hard to imagine. It combined all that was worst about the darkened age – there was no law, no regulation of the powerful, no true science, a wilful indulgence of excess and ignorance. They had retained scraps of knowledge, and put them to foul uses, giving them a veneer of military might. But it was fragile, and was already beginning to come apart even as we marched on it. I considered it like a great ash tree of the region's long-forgotten myths, its trunk iron-strong but its heart eaten away by rot. He knew it could be destroyed, even when other advisers counselled caution. So the order was given, and so, indeed, it transpired.

You asked for details. The campaign was one of the first in which we deployed significant numbers of the Legiones Cataegis alongside our regular troops. It was not their first engagement, but I believe it was the first in which an entire Legio was deployed. In this case, He chose the Fourth, given the cognomen at the time 'Iron Lords'. They were specialists in siegecraft, through both training and genecraft. Other Legiones, at that stage, had not reached full battle-readiness, but they were one of the first, and had impressed Him with their preparedness.

Alongside the Cataegis we were able to muster twenty-two regiments of standard troops. By then the Imperial Army was being organised into divisions by climatic zone, for the vagaries of the planet's weather were a major impediment to true global conquest, and we were able to call on cold-weather specialists. The majority of the forces we took with us were equipped with suitable armour and had access to modified weaponry. This was a necessity, rather than a luxury. Conditions were such that a human exposed to the elements without technological aid – or other, proscribed protective methods – died within hours. As I said, it was a hellish place. I often wondered what had enabled life to cling on there at all. We found our answer when we got there.

And then there was the Legio Custodes. Thirty warriors came with me, all assigned to protective duties. It was not anticipated that we would play the leading part in the fighting. Maulland Sen was, in many ways, a trial for the Cataegis. We wished to see if they could be as lethal en masse as they had already been in their smaller formations.

[You do not give them their familiar name.]

I can, if you wish me to. Thunder Warrior is merely the Low Gothic form.

[Tell me of their primarch.]

Their commander? I am not sure why you ask. Initially the fighting divisions had been envisaged as somewhat smaller than they eventually became, and thus the ranks were organised on orthodox regimental lines. The primarch was equivalent to the captain-general rank in broad terms, responsible for the discipline and conduct of the entire Legio. He was not physically different to any of his troops, but had distinguished himself in combat and leadership, and was appointed directly by the Emperor. His equipment was given particular attention, but you must remember that we were innovating all the time. Technologies were being rediscovered, or recreated, every year. Some troops were marching to war in fine armour, others were in generation-old fatigues. The primarchs and their command groups naturally were given the best of what we had. There were twenty of them in conception, one for each planned Legio, although by that stage not all had been given the title.

This primarch of the Fourth was Ushotan. He was a superlative warrior, and a fine general. In most respects, I admired him very much.

[Tell me of the fighting.]

You know the histories. They are accurate. Records of all the major engagements have been deposited within the Tower, and these are available to you. What more can I tell you?

[How it was to be there, as a witness.]

I see.

I take no pleasure, nor do I experience dismay, in combat. That was not the case with either our enemy or Ushotan's warriors. They were both ferocious. Our enemy was called the Priest-King. It was a name he had given himself, one which was perfectly appropriate. His followers were fanatical, deranged by both combat-narcotics and by the delusions he fed them. Somehow, even in that frigid waste, they had laid hands on technology from the forgotten age, and had learned, or been shown, how to use it. The results were despicable. We were fighting men stitched together into mockeries of the human form. Some were encased in machines, and goaded into war with pain amplifiers. Most of those we encountered, to one degree or another, had been shaped into new forms, swapping their dignity for a feral kind of strength.

The perimeter cities were conquered relatively quickly, for the taint of the Priest-King was lightest there, and the heartlands of the confederacy had always been inland, up in the high peaks where the skies flew with shards of wind-blown ice. We secured a beachhead on the south-western lowlands and flew in heavy landers to anchor our supply routes north. We were operating far from home, but had our familiar advantages – technology, confidence, energy. After only a month, we were planning our incursions further in.

As I have said, the terrain was always against us. The unen-hanced warriors suffered high rates of attrition, something that was hard to minimise. As we advanced north, many of them lost their minds. There were voices in the wind, and the cold was crushing. Those who died would be encountered again, ghosts in the gales, and it preyed on the nerves of our line troopers. We would not have been able to continue, had we only been able to draw on their services. This was not unforeseen, and underscored the necessity of the genecrafted detachments. I tell you this truly, for some are already beginning to doubt it – Terra could not have been conquered without them. We had fallen too far, and let too many monsters loose. They were the weapons that allowed us to advance into that ice-locked night.

So it was a hard contest, even if, with the Emperor with us, the outcome was never truly in doubt. Every citadel was contested, every offensive was met by a counter-offensive. They knew the conditions, they knew the pattern of the landscape, they had nowhere to withdraw to. More than seven thousand of our genecrafted shock troops died in the final assault. If you had seen how the Thunder Warriors fought, how committed they were and how unrestrained in slaughter, you would appreciate the nature of what we faced there.

Some of the weaknesses we displayed in Nordyc have now been addressed. All the armour we use now is of ceramic and metallurgical alloys, rather than the steel plate and hardened leather some of us wore back then. Our blades are equipped with energy fields, and the boltgun has replaced the old carbines and lasrifles. At Maulland Sen, in those days, the levels of technology were roughly comparable. What set us apart was our belief. The Priest-King had been hollowed out – his rantings were transparent even to those whom he had led into damnation – but we were led by Him. That, in the end, was always the difference, wherever we fought.

[But what was it like?]

Your pardon?

[What did it feel like, to be there?]

I am uncertain how to answer. I will do my best.

There was a… sickness. We could all taste it. I have encountered similar sensations since, when fighting other enemies of allied origin, but then it was new to me. It generated little but disgust in me and my brothers. For the Thunder Warriors under

Ushotan, it seemed to have a different effect. They thrived on it, at least for a time. They had, I surmised, the capacity to magnify whatever foulness they faced. That ferocity was useful, but it had its weaknesses. The walls around the final stronghold had been constructed in the mountains. The fortifications were set high and were well defended, and they had prepared for us over many years. I remember looking at it on the final night before the order was given to destroy it. It was lit from behind by a greenish light, and its black walls gleamed. There was an art to its construction, but a twisted one. Every angle of its immense defences seemed to embody pain, in one form or another. Set alongside the physical challenges, there was also the presence of other obstacles. Ghosts dogged us.

[You mean that figuratively, I presume?]

No. I use what seems to me the proper term.

It might have been wiser to slow the pace of the assault, to limit our eventual casualties, but by then the Cataegis were caught in a cycle of aggression. Death meant nothing to them. For a time, it seemed that orders meant nothing to them, either – they were elemental in their violence.

So I remember that city, lost in the dark and the ice at the edge of the world. The snow was piled up around it in drifts ten metres deep. Its high battlements were lined with flame weapons. When we assaulted, and brought up our own heavy guns, we created a flood of meltwater. We were advancing through torrents of it, a grey sea of filth that found its way inside our armour-seals. The tanks stalled, and the electrical relays burst. We were reduced to infantry engagements faster than anticipated, and still the walls were intact.

Ushotan made the first breakthrough. There was more slaughter than I would have countenanced, once he was inside. Not all the Priest-King's people were corrupted – some were slaves, and others might still have been salvaged for productive employment within the Imperium. In that, though, the Thunder Warriors demonstrated their greatest weakness. They were like the munitions we used back then – powerful, but unstable. Once loosed, they were hard to control. They broke through the inner chambers like a tide, slaughtering all they encountered. They demonstrated then the sheer power of the genecrafted soldier. If we had wished for an indication of their prowess, we could not have had a clearer one. And yet, so many had died, on both sides. It felt… wanton.

I spoke to Ushotan after the citadel had finally been taken, its roofs broken and its walls pounded into rubble. It was by then far into the following night – an entire diurnal cycle had passed in fighting, and we had barely looked up to notice it. I remember how his armour was, covered in already-freezing blood. His helm was gone, and his arm was broken. A fresh storm had descended, and the battlefields were buffeted with new snow, covering up the tracks of grey slush we had exposed.

He was laughing, when we met. He had a vivid light in his eyes. I thought he looked like the ghost of all murders.

[What did he say?]

He told me that he understood, for the first time, the reason he had been made. He told me that I would never feel the same way, and that he pitied me for that.

[Did you respond?]

I was troubled, as I recall. Not by the comment, nor the implied insult, but by the sentiment expressed. I felt as if we had unleashed something that would be hard to keep within bounds.

[Where did this feeling lead you?]

[Where did this feeling lead you, captain-general?]

-- Transcript ends --

SIX

'You did insult him,' said Armina.

'No, I don't think so.'

'But he cut things off, just then.'

Kandawire sighed. 'We were out of time. My fault. I shouldn't have arrived so late.'

The two of them walked briskly down the lumen-lit corridor, hurrying from the inner Council chambers towards the reception suites. Guards stood passively at the intersections, trying to look alert as a High Lord passed by. It was late, though, and the shifts were soon to switch over. The entire complex seemed semi-dormant, as if caught in half-slumber and now wondering how long it would be until dawn.

'He's given me another audience,' Kandawire said, as they turned into the long passageway leading down towards the inner gates.

'I thought you could demand as many as you liked?'

'I've never demanded anything,' Kandawire said. 'Now that

I've met him properly, it seems even more ludicrous than ever. I sense he wants to talk. Imagine that. I thought it would be like drawing blood from a stone.'

Armina hesitated, and they both came to a brief halt. 'I'll say it again. I don't understand what you hope to accomplish with this, even if you have as many hours as you need. We are already committed. We have been committed for months.'

'Not yet,' said Kandawire. 'We can still pull back, if we need to. I want to hear it, first, from his lips.' She smiled. 'It's procedure. Still a stickler for it.'

'When it suits you,' Armina said, under her breath, as they started to stride out again.

'I thought, somehow, he'd be... prouder. He talks like a man without pride. Imagine that, after all he's done.'

They reached an anteroom with two mail-clad guardians posted at the doors beyond. Kandawire gestured, and they pulled them open, revealing a plush room of fine fabrics and soft lumen-glare. A pair of long couches flanked a polished table, on which rested a half-drunk cup of recaff and a crumb-topped napkin. The man sitting on the left-hand couch looked the wrong size for his robes.

'Ophar,' said Kandawire, rushing up to him and taking him by both hands. 'Back safe. When you're away, I–'

The man smiled, nodding. 'Ai, kondedwa. Worry less. It was worth the trip.'

Armina sat primly in the background, and the guards shut them in again. Kandawire sat opposite Ophar, hitching her long skirts and shuffling forward. 'Tell me everything.'

He reached for the data-slate and handed it to her. 'All in here. Read it, if you wish to become sleepy. In case you don't wish to, here are the two things you need to know.'

Armina quietly reached up to her collar and activated a clandestine sweeper-baffle. Having listening devices in the Council chambers of the High Lords was unlikely, but not impossible; in its short life, the civilian administration of the Imperium had become almost as paranoid as the military. The only sign of her action was a slight tingle in the filtered atmosphere.

'First,' said Ophar, 'the observation of the Tower and Inner Walls. You were right. The Custodians are withdrawing from the main patrol routes, and concentrating on the Senatorum complex. I could not follow many of them, but they appear to be going somewhere underground. Literally, underground. I suspect there are chambers down there that none of us has access to. Quite why they need to gather there is mysterious. But, here's the thing – whatever the truth of that, it's clear to me that there are very few of them here. Tiny numbers, far fewer than I expected. Of course, we can't be sure. But I suspect, High Lord. I suspect that so many are fighting elsewhere, that the ones here are stretched to breaking. Perhaps that's why he's come back now? There will never be a better time, but it can't last.'

Kandawire nodded. 'Understood, though it would be folly to underestimate them. That creates a vacuum, which must be getting filled. What's doing that?'

'The Seneschals of the Departmento Regia Interior, as you'd expect. I've seen others drafted in south of the Senatorum. One new regiment – the Castellan Exemplars. Heard of them?'

'Never. The second thing?'

Ophar leaned forward, jabbing a long finger at the data-slate in Kandawire's hands. 'Small-arms, advanced type. Boltguns, personnel grenades, a lot of incendiaries. I can make little sense of the batch markings, but the quantities are there to see. Nothing like these is manufactured here. I have no idea at all where one could get hold of such things. All highly illegal, but it's been waved through. The crates are somewhere in the Palace now. That's your second problem.'

'As you predicted.' Kandawire sat back, and scanned through the data-slate's figures. 'And right on time.'

Armina looked at Ophar warily. 'Were you detected?'

Ophar shrugged. 'Who knows? It's said that they see every scrap of shadow under the sun. But I don't think so.' He turned to Kandawire. 'I do not think that you need any more reasons.'

Kandawire smiled wryly. 'Oh, I could do with many more. And more time.'

'They are already moving. This thing has started. If I were you, then–'

'You are not me, Ophar, and that is certainly for the best. I have another appointment with him.'

'I already voiced my concern about that,' interjected Armina.

'He wishes to keep you talking now,' said Ophar. 'Just more delays. He's no fool, and will not mistake you for one either.'

'I never thought he was,' said Kandawire. 'But I have my own reasons for wanting this. So little is known, even now, about where this all came from. It should come from his lips, if possible, and it is all being recorded.' She put the data-slate down and clasped her hands together. 'Evidence. A case. That is how it *must be done.*'

'Dangerous,' said Armina.

'He's a killer,' said Ophar. 'They say he can kill with a glance.'

Kandawire snorted. 'Nonsense.'

'You are hesitating, kondedwa. If I had done so, back then, we would never have made it out of Afrik. Remember that lesson.'

Kandawire shot him an irritated glance, and for a moment, she was that little girl again, too spoiled to be fearful, irritated at leaving her vids behind as the world burned. Then the expression melted away, revealing older, harder features. 'I have enough to give the signal. But they can be called back, any time.'

'Any time,' said Armina.

'Any time,' said Ophar.

The chamber fell silent. From somewhere, everywhere, the low hum of machinery filtered through the thick walls. They never rested, those machines, building, building, building.

Kandawire looked up at the whitewashed ceiling. Even here, right at the heart of the most powerful empire the world had ever known, the cracks were already visible. It was all happening too fast, and things were not setting right.

'Very well,' she said, softly. 'Tell them to begin.'

Liora Harrad had been in the Dungeon for six hours, and the extended shift was getting to her.

She lifted her hand, encased in a translucent layer of antibacterial synthskin, and observed the minor tremble there. She was hungry. She was tired. Still, she could hardly leave her post yet, not without authorisation from Ilaed.

She let her hand fall again, and glanced from side to side, down the rows of technicians at their cell-like stations – four thousand, in both directions. Not for the first time, she wondered what she was doing there among them.

It was not a real dungeon. They all called it that, however, for the old tropes were present and correct – stone walls blotched with algae and damp; heavy archways sunk in darkness; thick flags on the floors, all uneven, many cracked. Liora had no idea when the place had been built, but it was clearly a very long time ago.

It was a long way down. It took her over an hour to travel by turbo-lift from the upper reaches of the secure workers' compound, through the many levels of increasing darkness and secrecy, before finally the mouldering heart of the Dungeon welcomed her for another day of toil.

The daily journey was like travelling in time. You started at the top, where the gleaming walls were being raised in defiance of the climate and altitude, all gold and alabaster to catch the blaze of the unveiled sun. Then you were descending fast through the pre-Imperial zones, piled atop one another in blocks of cracking rockcrete, and the light began to fade, giving way to rows of industrial lumen-banks. A little further, and then you were truly underground, sliding along transit shafts on chain transports and glimpsing the flicker of under-hab levels in the dark. There were many things tantalisingly beyond view – the foundations of the mighty reactors that kept the growing city supplied with power, the water processors, the waste caverns with their endlessly rotating purifier turntables. Tunnel entrances opened, gaping invitingly, but with no signage or proper illumination it was impossible to know where they led.

Down, down, down. The enclosed atmosphere warmed up, and travellers in the conveyer cages shed their cold-weather gear. There were security stops, a dozen of them. The initial checkpoints were manned by Seneschals of the Departmento Regia Interior. The guards became more fearsome the further you went, until, right at the bottom, they were the gold-plumed mortal servants of the Tower itself. Now and again, the process would even be supervised by one of the Custodian Guard themselves, towering silently over the queues of technician-caste workers seeking entrance to the Dungeon precincts.

They scared Liora. They scared everyone. That was their function, of course – to loom in the shadows, saying nothing, doing nothing, just watching. On the rare occasions they moved, their armour whispered with a spectre-hum of perfectly aligned machinery. They smelled faintly of ritual incense. In this hyper-rational Imperium, they were throwbacks to a mystical past, possessed of such raw physical prowess that it daunted the soul just to contemplate it.

And then, beyond the last sentinel station, was the Dungeon. Its size was similarly daunting – an entire city buried in the roots of the mountains, lightless save for its constellations of floating suspensor lumens, themselves poised over deeper shafts that carried on down, seemingly towards the heart of the planet itself. Some of the chambers were of standard human dimensions, others were truly cyclopean. All were humid, cloying and scored hard with age. Breathing that heavy air felt like ingesting the dust of innumerable generations, locked away down here while the world above burned with unleashed atomics, hibernating in safety, planning, building, waiting for the moment to emerge again.

Liora sighed. She rolled her shoulders. The station in front of her looked much as it always did – racks of dishes and vials, glowing softly from the photosensitive chems in the solutions. A micro-cogitator chattered away, producing a narrow ream of marked archive-parchment. Her analyser lenses tilted in from the right-hand side, the injectors and the centrifuges from the left. Comm-tubes snaked around her, each loaded with vacuum canisters ready for despatch to the laboratorium collator hoppers. Mecha-arms twitched overhead, hung from the rails that ran the length of the echoing hall, ready to scoop up burdens and clatter them down the long trails towards the incubators.

All around her, technicians were working. Their backs were curved, their hands busy, their faces hidden behind refractive clusters of zoom-lenses. Transistor-beads hummed with static electricity. Every so often, snatches of it would skip and flicker down the long aisles, briefly illuminating the coal-black vaults above. The space stank of ammonia, and vents of steam curled from wheezing atmospheric scrapers.

She looked back at the dish in front of her, clamped in place with brass arms, studded with a dozen calibrated injectors and sensor-bulbs. She considered the contents, its flaws and its virtues, and what could be done about the former while preserving the latter. She reset the amniotic layer, ready to run the charge through it again.

Sanguinary obsessive trait B, she inputted onto the cogitator's mind-wafer. *Will attempt to rectify. Again.*

Before she could depress the lever, a pulse kicked into her temple-set comm-bead. She considered ignoring it – the research was at a delicate stage – but then remembered what was at stake. She cancelled the injection, pulled the electrodes out of the solution precursor and flooded the dish with refrigerant. Then she checked the secure transmission.

'I received your request,' came Ilaed's thin voice. 'Very well, if you must. But be quick.'

So he'd agreed. Good. There had never been any guarantees.

'Complying,' she sent back, and pushed away from the station. It took a few moments to decouple her neural plugs, and then she was walking down the long aisle, her shoes clicking on the stone floor.

No one watched her go. The rows of faces, hundreds of them, remained fixed at their stations, illuminated by pale blotches from below. The only sounds were the scratch of auto-quills, the clicking of the machines, the faint bubbling of the amniotic tubes. The atmosphere was reverent. Almost religious.

Ironic, she thought.

Liora reached the outer portal, submitted herself to the security sweep, then went to the pulse-shower chambers to shed her protective gear and change into her standard uniform. As ever, when she peeled the synthskin from her hands, the flesh underneath was puffy and livid with irritation. She stepped through the scanners, pressed her fingertip to the pheromone reader, waited patiently for the blood-sample needles.

Then she was out, still within the Dungeon confines, but beyond the steel-trap perimeter that guarded the chambers where the real work was actually done. The guards were still numerous, as were her fellow technicians, but the surveillance level dropped a fraction. She looked up, to where ranked standards of the Raptor Imperialis hung listlessly in the humid air. It got to you, after a while, being enclosed all the time, never seeing the open sky. She had heard stories of technicians going mad, having to be dragged off by the attendants, never to be seen again. She had even considered how possible it would be to fake an episode, just to see where all the invalids ended up. Of course, she had her great purpose now, and that made the monotony bearable.

She walked with surety, for the readiest way to attract attention was to give the slightest hint of uncertainty. Gradually, the crowds thinned out. She was heading for the lower storage depots, where flesh-and-blood adepts were increasingly outnumbered by lumbering, wafer-automated forklifts. Some of those spaces were huge, and you couldn't even see the roof from the floor. Some were off limits and sealed with heavy blast doors. Every inch of it all was drenched in paranoia and need-to-know mysteriousness – the subterranean city of secrets.

She reached her destination – a nondescript metal portal with the usual range of security seals and retinal-scan appendages. She slunk into the door-well, pressing herself up against the inner edge.

'Here now,' she pulsed over the direct link. 'Access, please.'

It took a while for the command to come through – no doubt they all had to go carefully, too. Then, one by one, the locks slid open. The scanner blinked out, and the seals broke. Liora pushed the access panel lightly, and the door hissed open. She slipped inside, and the perfect dark slid over her as the door closed her in.

She stood for a moment in the shadow, waiting for her breathing to subside. She could already smell some of what she had come to find – stacked up neatly, ready for inspection. The only remaining task was to check the manifests were accurate – this was the last batch, and so after that everything would be ready to go.

Then, for some reason, she sniffed. It should have been musty in that chamber, clogged with the stale air that filled every storeroom on the level, but there was something else. Something like... incense.

Before she knew anything more, lumens came on, flaring like torches. She tried to scrabble back through the door, but the locks seemed to have jammed tight. She blinked, only making the dazzle worse. Despite that, she was able to notice two important, and unexpected, things.

First, the chamber was empty of its expected cargo. There were no storage crates on the floor, though from the scratches on the rockcrete it looked as though something had been there at one stage.

Second, she was not alone. The other occupant was gigantic, a third taller than her and far bulkier. Even blurred by her watering eyes, she could see just what had been caged in here with her, and it made her want to gag with terror.

'Technician Liora Harrad, Class Tertius,' said Samonas calmly, keeping his usual civilised distance. 'I think it is time that you and I spoke candidly.'

SEVEN

Night, out in the wastes. The land was sandy and flat, a blasted bowl of scrub and dust that got in the teeth and made the skin itch. The stars shone vividly above, untempered by light pollution, a pinprick mess of ivory against the deep ground of the void. The moon was a waning crescent, making the distant hills a soft blue-blush under the dark.

Achilla limped up the rise, feeling his joints – both original and mechanical – ache. His fatigues hung a little too loosely over his frame, these days. Once he had bulked out his battle-kit well enough. He'd looked good in it, and that had meant a lot to him. Things were meant to be more civilised these days, but he had always found truth in the old adage that girls liked a soldier. He'd been a lot of places, a lot of encampments, shifting with the campaigns that never seemed to truly stop, and it had been plenty of fun. Despite all the changes, a few things remained constant in war – the alcohol, the boredom, the time to kill. And between those lulls, spent in shot-dives and amasec-dens with an arm around someone friendly, there was the sudden thrill of it all kicking off again.

Achilla liked fighting very much. In the earliest days he'd done it for money, giving him what he needed to buy those few good augmetics from the flesh-stitchers in the Mumbay-Rashstra combines. For a long time that had been good business, and all he'd needed to do was stay alive. His right eye was an oculus-targeter, his right hand was underpinned by a tungsten core, and both legs had been stripped out and rebuilt with musculo-dermal boosters. He'd resisted getting pain-dampeners threaded into his nervous system, because they dampened pleasure too, and that had been more of a priority in those days.

Those had been the good times. Wars were frequent, short and localised. No one had enough power to stamp out anyone else, not properly, and so everything was a matter of skirmishing and burning – quickly over, quickly paid for. He couldn't remember when it had started to change. Someone a long time ago had told him of an emperor from the south – or maybe the west – who was steadily chewing up the little kingdoms. It might have been Yulia, or maybe Elenora, but whoever it was he hadn't paid much attention, for there were always stories of emperors chewing up the little kingdoms, whether out of wishful thinking or dread, depending on your perspective.

This time, though, it had been a real one. Work started to dry up, and for the first time Achilla had to travel to find it. Borders started to be drawn, ones with watchtowers and patrols. The parameters of life got smaller, just as the fighting got harder and less fun. Armies started appearing with much smarter uniforms and much bigger guns. Worst of all, they were being paid not by results, but as professionals.

After nearly dying in that business off the Arabyn Depression, there had been some serious thinking to do. It turned out that most people hadn't really liked soldiers at all – they had just been the ones with the coin and the weapons – and so things had got perilous. There was a mood of vengeance in the air. The good times were thought of, by worrying numbers of individuals, as really bad times, and there were stories of lynchings doing the rounds.

So Achilla did what he'd always done, and adapted. He went east, then north, keeping his augmetics wrapped up and out of view, slowly running down his coin reserves from the last big job and looking for a way out. Everywhere he went, it was the same story – the Emperor, the Emperor, the Emperor. The more he travelled, the more his eyes were opened. They were building things again – cities, ports, factories. The little kingdoms really were falling, toppling faster every year, their resources and their populace swallowed up into this great beast of an empire that seemed to be suddenly everywhere at once.

The Imperium, they were calling it. There was a whole language being resurrected with it, full of baffling ranks and stations, and a single icon flying on a thousand different standards – an eagle's head, ringed by lightning. People seemed to like that emblem. Where those standards flew, the dull hand of order was restored.

It was a grim spectacle, but not one to be challenged, at least for the time being. Achilla found an Imperial regiment recruiting in the industrial zone of the Rohinj hyper-conurb, and spent the very last of his coin scrubbing out the worst signs of his past life. He needn't have bothered with that, it turned out – the requirement for soldiers was almost inexhaustible, and the officers paid very slack attention to where their recruits came from. They had little choice, to be fair, for Terra was awash with lots of Achillas, all of whom looked much the same as one another and had the same dreary stories to tell.

So the fighting started up again. It wasn't as entertaining now, as he had to slot into battalions and follow orders. Still, he got paid. He saw more of the world, which was being moulded and remade at such a rate that no one knew quite what to think about it, save those terrifying warriors of the new Imperium who strode across its bounds like gold-clad sentinels of a forgotten age.

Achilla even saw one of them once, from a distance. He should have been concentrating on his own fighting – advancing up the course of a dried-out irrigation canal to assault a derelict pumping station – but once you caught a glimpse of one of those golden devils, everything else seemed slightly pointless. He'd used his old augmetics to get a better view, and so from a range of almost three kilometres he'd watched the whole thing unfold.

He couldn't even count the number of enemies that it had killed. He couldn't even really see how it was doing it, the pace was so fast. The devil wasn't using a gun, like anyone sensible, but some kind of electricity-wrapped spear. It was carving through solid stone, slashing through the masonry as if it weren't there. A rusty old tank was kicked over – *kicked over* – and then pulled into shreds of burning metal.

Achilla found himself appalled. That level of naked power was... unfair. There could be no enjoyment in it. There was no chance that the other one might strike a lucky blow. There was no indication at all that any money was changing hands with those things, which was an aberration – fighting for its own sake, without a decent reward for services rendered, was the most perverse inclination of all.

So he'd turned the augmetic off, and got back to what he was supposed to be doing. And yet, he never forgot. In the cities, they were flying those eagle-head banners and celebrating the return of civilisation, but out there, in the deserts and the ruins, at the sharp end, monsters were being set loose. It didn't matter that they were clad in gold and crimson, that they looked like something noble and refined, because *nothing* noble and refined could do those things. It was a sham, and Achilla knew all about those, because he'd been on the other end of them more often than not.

He kept his head down, after that. He went where he was told. He didn't pay too much attention to the names and the places, for the less you knew the better. He started to drink to forget, not for fun, and that had predictable consequences. He aged. His implants started to ache. His story, as ignoble as it was, was most evidently coming to an end.

He drifted into the margins. It turned out that there were others who didn't entirely appreciate the way things were going. Some were malcontents and thieves, some were mad; others were like him and had never really fitted in anywhere. Others, he discovered, had more thoroughgoing concerns. Slowly, by a process he was barely aware of, he found himself right on the edge, ripe for the whispers that still ran through the rapidly cleaning air, if you knew where to listen.

Loyalty was a strange thing, Achilla thought to himself. He'd never thought of himself as loyal to anything much, and yet, here he was, back where he had started, doing what he'd done all those many years ago. Now, the danger was greater. Far greater. The chances of him surviving the year were slimmer than they'd ever been. Still, at least he was having fun again. That was the important thing.

He slipped, his ankle twisting over a rock as he limped to the crest of the rise. He leaned on his jag-rifle – an archaic weapon almost as tall as he was – and caught his breath. The air was cold, and would get rapidly colder as the night deepened.

Below him, spread out in the rift valley below, was the forward detachment. The night air tasted of promethium, and thrummed with the low growl of hundreds of engines idling. Sodium lamps twinkled amid the dark hulks, betraying the movement of thousands of infantry marching. On the side, protected by twin lines of heavy armour, the supply transports waited silently. Seeker drones prowled overhead, black as pitch and near silent.

Achilla felt a pulse at his neck. Sniffing, he reached for the tracker at his belt. His thumb moved stiffly over the ident patch, betraying that curse of age. It took a moment for the comms coil to clear out, and then it was glowing – a simple message, one they had been waiting weeks for.

He stared at it, checking that it was definitely the right one. He felt his creaking heart pick up, beating harder, just like the old days. His leathery face cracked into a smile.

<Proceed> the tracker told him. Out across the rift valley, thousands of trackers would be saying the same thing.

Right on cue, hundreds of engines coughed into smoggy life. The drones whined down low, ready to be stowed away in their carriers. Vehicle headlights flared out, casting long pools of dirty gold across the moonlit steppe.

We're doing it, he told himself, happily, limping down the slope towards his own carrier. As he went, he double-checked the power-unit on his rifle, and the act itself gave him a surge of pleasure.

The first transports were already moving out. It would take hours just to clear the staging point, such was the volume gathered here – cast-offs, renegades, ne'er-do-wells of all kinds, bolstered by the true believers – but the journey would feel like a short one.

We're doing it, thought Achilla, hurrying to join his unit, never even knowing, nor caring, where the order had come from, for such things had never mattered to him, only the essential core of it.

On the march again. Just as it ought to be.

* * *

In the beginning, there had been no High Lords.

The empire, in its earliest days, had only required generals, and few enough of those. The Emperor had always been present, and He was the central star around which all else revolved. For many, the Emperor and the Imperium were virtually synonymous, the one a reflection of the other. That was a simplification, but it captured one essential truth – that without Him, there were no substantial differences between this new power and all the other ones that had briefly risen to prominence before. In the language of the old logicians, the Emperor was a necessary component of the Imperium, though hardly sufficient.

Then, of course, there was Malcador. Malcador and the Emperor, the Emperor and Malcador. No one knew who had come first. The rumours were legion. Some said that Malcador had been the Emperor's very first gene-creation. Others said that they were twins, one gifted power and the other gifted cunning. Others said that Malcador had travelled the Earth collecting shards of a greater whole, and had created the Emperor as a gestalt being of infinite power. Rumours persisted that shamanic rites had been conducted, though by whom, to whom and with whom was never easy to determine. Many half worshipped Malcador. Many more secretly hated and feared him, and told stories that he whispered lies into the Emperor's ear in order to keep the poor downtrodden and seize riches for himself.

With Malcador, the only thing that was certain was that he knew the stories, had a hand in spreading them, and was careful to ensure they were all false. The essence of Malcador was that he had no essence – he was a shadow, a memory, a pale reflection of the greater soul who walked beside him. His power, which was colossal in itself, was that of deflection and uncertainty. The Emperor would level a mountain with a word of truth. Malcador would erode it over a thousand years of lies.

Then came Valdor, the golden champion. Though a member of the triumvirate in appearance, in truth he was the servant to the others. He was the standard bearer, the cup-holder, the skull-bringer. If there were doubts about the origins of the two principals, there was none about him – Valdor had been made, created from mortal Terran stock. Perhaps there had been other captains-general, or failed attempts to create one, but he had been the one that had lasted. He had been the one that had set the template, afterwards never broken, for the Legio Custodes. If Valdor had been a different man, perhaps the Custodians would have been different, too. He was dour, reserved, quietly spoken, intelligent and dry. So were they all, too. Maybe that was the result of the manner of their creation, or maybe that was the influence of their captain. Nature, nurture. Even for demigods, the old debates could still rage.

Below those three, for a long time, there had been nothing. Soldiers, scientists, builders, artisans, yes, but no statesmen, no counsellors. They were not needed, at the start, for who could compare with this original trio of supernaturals? What advice would such leviathans take from the unwashed mass of a cowed and brutal humanity?

It was only when the first cities fell that things began to change. An army conquers, an administration rules. From the outset, the Emperor's intentions were plain – to return to the methods of the past, to impose the law, to banish superstition and religion, to usher in a new age of discovery. The Imperium's subjects first numbered in their thousands, then their hundreds of thousands, then their millions. Not even the mightiest of warlords could have ruled over so many unaided.

So, to begin with, there were the Magisters Temporal, the rulers of provinces, tasked with ensuring taxation and security once the armies had rolled on to new conquest. These were soon supplemented by regional Lords Civilian, who assumed responsibility for the expanding clusters of provinces. For a period, almost seventy years, this system creaked along, only ever barely coping with the many demands of a growing populace. There were food riots in Asia-Majoris, currency runs in the Yndonesic Bloc, and a continual festering sore of intermittent unrest and sedition everywhere else. The Emperor was at war the whole time, or secreted away on His many scientific programmes, and so could not be spared for every petty dispute and uprising.

Once the Palace had been constructed in outline and the capital of the Imperium settled in Himalazia, more lasting roots could be set down. Standards of governance drawn up, so it was said, by Malcador, were given form as part of the initial precepts of the Lex Pacifica. The Lords Civilian became the second tier of command, overseen by four 'High' Lords Civilian, each with responsibility, not for a geographical domain, but an area of government: the Lord Commander Militant of the Imperial Armies, the Master of the Administratum, the Provost Marshal of the Divisio Arbites and the Chancellor of the Estate Imperium. It was unknown at that stage, even by the individuals in question, whether such an arrangement would last, or if it would be swept away or modified by the tides of change, but for the time being, the highest tier of authority below the Emperor's direct rule had been established.

Some ancient patterns were not adopted. There was never a democratic mandate, for the world was too perilous to allow the masses to sway the direction of travel. This was always a dictatorship, headed by a single individual, but with the promise of benign governance at its heart. The High Lords were not figureheads, and nor were they powerless. As the Emperor swept across the old ruined continents at the head of His genhanced armies, it fell to them to allocate scarce resource, to oversee the operation of the law enforcers, to reconstruct all that had been wilfully cast aside by more slipshod generations.

As Noum Retraiva, the first Master of the Administratum, said, 'They are the sword, we are the quill. There is an old saying, concerning the relative might of each, but I forget its precise formulation.'

They had all had tortuous paths to their high station. Retraiva had always been born to rule – he was descended from one of the old purebred families of Merica's atomics-shattered west coast, and had fantastic wealth. It had been an easy choice for him to throw in with the new Imperium, for power always recognised power. He had brought with him the core of nine full-strength armoured regiments and whole vaults of valuable tech, and some reward had to be offered for that. He was a cynical man, with an eye for personal enrichment, but also fearsomely rigorous. Under his auspices, the capability of the Administratum grew swiftly, taking on hundreds of officials, or 'adepts' as the Gothic increasingly had it.

Pelops Dravagor, the Chancellor of the Estate Imperium, was Retraiva's creature. Kli-San Weia, the Lord Commander Militant, was Malcador's. That left the Provost Marshal, highest authority on the Lex and master of the also-rapidly-expanding Arbites network. For some reason, as a result of switchback machinations that even Kandawire found hard to recall in all their detail, the post had gone not to an old-school potentate like Retraiva, nor to a career lackey like Dravagor, but to a refugee from Afrik making a name for herself in Himalazia's chaotic tribunals and arbitration cells.

Uwoma Kandawire, Provost Marshal. The title still felt odd, almost like a joke that had not yet had its punchline. Within her stubby fingers she held the implementation of all law, the imposition of order and the suppression of civil eruption. Expectation, perhaps, would have led to an authoritarian soul taking over, but Kandawire had never been that.

'When the wars are done,' she had said to Malcador, years ago, before the position had been confirmed and they were merely acquaintances, 'history tells us the victorious army turns on the people. What shields them? Weapons? They have none. Only the civilian power. Only the law.'

'This army upholds the law,' Malcador had said, softly, sounding amused.

'For now,' Kandawire had replied, staring right into the Sigillite's creased and parched face. 'But the conquest will end, one day. Then what?'

'Where did you learn this history?'

From old vid-books, taken from the burning edge of Afrik – that had been the only answer. The Sigillite could scoff at that as much as he liked. Perhaps he'd lived long enough to remember the old glories first-hand, but she knew that what her father had told her was how it was. It had always been the case, and always would be, no matter how benign and munificent this Emperor was supposed to be.

The warrior is the servant of the worker.

And so she was now on the way to the Tower again, to test the resilience of that mantra. Storm clouds had come in hard from the west over the Palace, throwing a dirty hail across the construction sites. Heavy crawlers and cranes wallowed in freezing mud-slicks, their cargoes lashed by slush-bearing winds. The storm felt like a heavy one in the making. There were often such storms, boiling out of the clear air and vomiting their fury onto the fragile shells of this brave new capital. Through it all, the construction would continue. The techwrights would batten down, set their iron-bound jawlines and keep going. One way or another, the city would carry on rising.

The flyer struggled in the gale, its viewports streaked with grey runnels. The marker lights at the landing pad were bleary and indistinct, washed out by the hammer-pattern hail.

Callix ushered her to the chamber, just as before. And just as before, the conversation was inconsequential.

'Inclement weather,' the adjutant had said.

'Yes, frightfully so,' Kandawire had replied, wondering if sarcasm registered with these people.

And then everything had melted away again, as it had done the last time, leaving the stone-hard chamber, the smooth marble, the echoing voids. No sun bathed that stone now, and the windows opened up onto a maelstrom of grey, shrouding the towers on the horizon.

'A significant storm,' said Valdor, greeting her with a nod.

He was entirely unchanged. His mood never seemed to alter. Here he was again, gigantic, clad in those simple robes that seemed to amplify rather than contain his extraordinary physical presence, and speaking in that scholarly, precise manner that made her want to scream.

'We're used to them, up here,' Kandawire said, taking her place without being asked.

Valdor sat opposite her, his spine ramrod straight. 'I am sure you are. This, though, will be a test.'

There seemed little need for preliminaries, this time around. It was still hard to look Valdor in the eye – something about that preternatural calmness was almost infinitely intimidating – but the parameters had already been set.

She had given the order, though. Somewhere out to the west, the convoys were moving. Did he know? Were there any limits to what he could detect? If so, predictably, he gave no sign.

'Are you willing to begin?' she asked.

'Of course.'

'I have a different topic in mind, this time. A rumour. One that may have no substantial truth to it, but it has reached my ears from more than one source.'

'Intriguing.'

'You spoke to me of Ushotan,' Kandawire said. 'You indicated that there were known issues with the primarchs of the Thunder Legion, as well as with the troops. I have been privy to information about a new programme, one of enhanced leadership for the Imperial armies, that was kept secret from the Council, precisely to correct this. New generals, if you will.'

'What provenance did this… information have?'

'Nothing solid, as you'd expect. I have never known what to make of it, and the administration of the army is hardly my concern.' She swallowed, feeling her throat drying out. 'But, given what you told me of the Cataegis primarchs, I wondered if there was anything the High Council ought to be made aware of.'

'So, is that the start?'

'Yes, if you are willing.'

'You are mistaken, I am afraid, High Lord. There are no new generals for the Imperial Army. But I am aware, of course, of the incident that spawned these rumours. Activate your recording device, and I will tell you of it.'

EIGHT

-- Transcript begins--
[Thank you. When did the incident take place?]
Twenty-six years ago.
[In the Palace?]
That is classified.
[Ah.]

I have perfect recall. You know that? Nothing, since the day I awoke following my creation into this newer, higher state, is hidden from me. Names, faces, actions – they are all vivid, as real as when they first entered my life. But even if that were not so, I would remember that day with absolute clarity. It is burned on my mind like a brand. I see the events of it in my sleep. Even when waking, the sensation is never far away.

[What sensation?]

Of falling. Falling through a hole in the universe, unable to catch at the edges. Now I see you smiling again. It is the truth. I have never considered myself an artful user of language.

[Perhaps, then, from the beginning?]

I was with the Sigillite. The Lord Malcador. We were discussing the very thing you raised with me. You will recall my concerns about the Cataegis during the Maulland Sen campaign. Those concerns had not gone away during the following century of their many deployments. We had conquered much of the globe by then, with the Thunder Warriors bearing the brunt of the fighting, so do not think we were unmindful of their sacrifice. By then, it was widely believed that what could have been perfected, had been perfected. A Thunder Warrior was a truly fearsome proposition. They were armed and armoured nearly as well as the Legio Custodes. Their numbers had grown rapidly, following improvements in the gene-cultivating methods used here and at the other sites.

But it was never enough. They remained unstable. From primarch to neophyte, they would break down suddenly, or lose their minds, or simply stop responding to orders. This was not simply a matter of dry practicality for us – it was a foul thing to witness. A warrior's blood might suddenly rebel against the arteries that carried it, or the organs might start to devour themselves, or the muscle might explode with breakneck growth. For a proud and fearless creation, that was a poor way to die.

Be aware, also, that they were quite conscious of this likely outcome. It did predictable things to their psychology. Knowing that they were limited by time and circumstance, their attitude to risk became even more cavalier. They were hard to govern from the start, but as the Imperium began to reach its secure zenith, they risked becoming an empire within an empire, and one with the old reckless dangers of the past writ large.

That was the subject I had come to speak with Malcador about. We had met many times in the past, on some occasions in the presence of the Emperor Himself, to debate the same issue. This time, however, our council was not with Him, but with the foremost practitioner of gene-arts in the entire Imperium. You will know the name, of course – I am speaking of Astarte.

[Amar Astarte.]

Quite. The three of us had gathered to consider something that had been developing, under His auspices, for a number of years. A way to bring order to the situation. We had won our empire through the application of gene-science. We all believed that its weaknesses could also be purged through the application of gene-science. Every victory achieved by our armies was matched by a victory in the underground laboratories established by the Emperor. It is important to understand how essential this programme was, and how difficult. We were working with fragments and splinters of ancient knowledge, most of it lost centuries ago and only preserved at all thanks to His tireless efforts. The complexity of it was prodigious. It required a vast expenditure of resources. Each time we recovered priceless technology during an engagement, it was brought back and pressed into service towards the ultimate goal – a solution to the problem of genetic instability.

On occasion, I am asked why it has taken so long to bring this one world to heel. I am tempted to reply that no other conqueror has had to forge his weapons while at the same time waging his war. Victory begat victory, in the end, but it was never easy.

Our meeting, that day, was required due to certain disagreements over the correct course of action at that stage. The Sigillite had been involved closely with the Emperor's labours, and advocated a radical course, or so it seemed to me at any rate. The Lord Malcador had, and has, great faith in genecraft. Our only failing, he argued then, was that we had not gone as far as we might have done.

I felt differently. I had not learned to have the same

unwavering faith in the processes we used. Mass production of genecrafted warriors is fraught with pitfalls. We in the Order are biologically altered, of course, but with us the procedure is singular and painstaking. It would never suffice to supply an entire army this way, or else the productive capacity of the Imperium would be unable to generate anything else. I was nevertheless of the view that the Custodians were, at that point, capable of overseeing the Imperium's next phase of growth, bolstered by the far larger armies of unenhanced troops we then possessed. That was the central point of our disagreement.

[And Astarte?]

Astarte is an official. She is a genius, of course, but her craft is science, not policy. She regarded herself as a servant of the Emperor. To be more precise, I think she regarded herself as a manifestation of the Emperor's intentions.

I should remark on this. There are those who claim, foolishly, that the Imperium is the result of one man's efforts. An extraordinary man, to be sure, but a singular entity nonetheless. This is a profoundly dangerous assumption. As we saw for ourselves on many occasions, once the cult of the individual reaches a certain point, it becomes impossible to restrain attributions of godhood. This was always a danger, given the many demagogues in the Terran past, and so the Emperor was mindful to distribute duties among those who were skilful enough to comprehend His vision. His greatest gift, I think, is to be alive to the possibilities of those who serve Him. He takes keen delight in the intelligent human mind, and will protect those in whom He sees potential. So it is that the Imperium is the product of many souls, all working towards one vision.

Astarte is one of these. Save for the Emperor Himself, no one alive on this world understands the ways of gene-manipulation more than her. We have never been close in counsel, due to our differing functions, but I yield to no one in my admiration of her.

[What was the result of the conference?]

There was no result. It was curtailed before any conclusion could be determined.

[You hesitate. Do you wish to continue?]

This is the moment that is seared on my mind. I am considering how best to tell it.

Consider the situation. We were deep in the foundations of what is now becoming the Inner Palace. This had ever been the heart of our operations, and much of it remains tightly restricted. It is the Sigillite's domain, in all but name – his ancient order delved that place, and populated it with their artefacts. Other chambers were carved out, in close proximity to the older caverns. In large part, this was to provide access to machinery the Sigillite had been instrumental in preserving. Otherwise, I believe symbolism played a more important role. We were, as we saw it, reviving humanity, so we started, as we had to, close to its oldest remnants.

There were other places. Some of them, only the Emperor knew of. Some we were all familiar with. Some were close at hand, others very far away, all of them chosen according to the dimensions of the greater project. There was another location, one that I still cannot reveal to you with any precision, only that it was far from here. So far that, when the alarms began, we were a long way from where we needed to be.

I have often speculated on whether things would have been different, had I been closer. I believe Malcador feels the same way, and it is a source of some guilt for both of us that we were not there. However, the Emperor was at the very heart of it, and if He was unable to intervene successfully then I must believe that no one could have had the power to prevent what happened.

We acted as swiftly as we could. We were like a storm breaking. I summoned all that I could of the Legio, and we travelled to the forbidden centre. All thoughts of secrecy were gone: in that instant, we tore the skies apart to reach our destination. Malcador came with us, as did Astarte. I can still remember my desperation to be faster. I believe I came as close as I will ever come to knowing *fear* in those moments, not for myself, but for something far greater.

By the time we arrived, the entire facility was in a state of confusion. The walls were breaking, the roofs were coming down. Buttresses that had taken years to fashion were twisting out of shape under sudden loads. There were bodies everywhere – technicians, artificers, mech-workers. Even Custodians had been slain, though by means that I could not understand, for their armour was still intact.

We were soon deep underground, caked in grey dust and fighting against the darkness and the smoke. The halls were of considerable size. Tens of thousands laboured in that facility, all under a cloak of the most stringent secrecy, and the survivors were panicking, trapped in the corridors like herd animals in a slaughterhouse.

The Emperor was not visible to me, but I understood why. The entire structure of that place had been critically damaged, and He was holding it together. Though I could not determine His precise location, without Him the chambers would have by then have been nothing more than choked rubble. It was a strange sensation, moving through a physical volume of space entirely suffused by the Emperor's presence. It was also a reminder to me of His power. Even I need reminders of that, from time to time.

So. The more I saw, the more I felt dread reaching for me. You remember what I said about the sickness at Maulland Sen? The same sensation was there, only many times more concentrated.

I saw seasoned soldiers vomiting blood, or dashing their heads against the rock. Every lumen was flickering, casting the blood-stains in patterns of failing light. It was hard to breathe, even with our physiology and armour protection.

The deeper we went, the more horror we witnessed. It was far worse than Maulland Sen, for this was in a place we had carved out ourselves. It was deemed safe, as secure as any mortal power could make. That was another lesson for us – there are no safe places.

[Where was this? What had happened to it?]

I cannot tell you everything. You will understand more in due course.

We hastened to recover what could be recovered. I directed those of my order to impose their control on the outer precincts, and this was slowly achieved. They were compelled to euthanise many whose minds had been turned by what they had seen. Those who might yet survive were taken to medical units. Emergency engineering teams were shuttled in to shore up the outer gates, lest we end up buried alive within as we laboured. Every one of them was accompanied by a Custodian, for there was still madness singing in the air, and I could only trust those of my own kind to remain resistant to it.

I began to understand the true nature of what we were set against, then. The Priest-King was just a shard cut from this dark crystal, a mere sliver of a greater abomination. I could breathe it in, there. I could taste its essence, like wyrmwood on my tongue. On some days, even now, I can still taste it.

The greatest of the many chambers was, by then, lost to us. Its interior was aflame, its great vials broken. I looked inside, just for a split second, and saw twenty vessels robbed of their contents, with lightning still snapping from vane to vane. There was nothing to be done there, and I almost turned away from the deeper vaults too. It was Astarte who pressed on, and I followed her. There was more to salvage, she said, and I instantly saw that she was correct.

Further down, in long galleries cut from the living rock, were the secondary repositories. Imagine it – walls over fifty metres high, running back beyond sight into the heart of the darkness, all lined with vials in precisely categorised sections. The vaults were temperature controlled, though I could already feel the ambient climate rising rapidly. Some of the caddies looked badly damaged, with glass broken or electro-seals malfunctioning. If they had been left there much longer, they would all have burned.

Astarte was invaluable in those moments. She knew which caches to retrieve and which would have to be left. I pressed every available member of my order into service, for all the technicians on that level were dead or missing. One by one, we extracted the caches and took them to places of safety. We kept records of all that we took, and made sure that none of those retrieved went missing. The two of us, Astarte and I, spent that desperate time working together. We did not speak much, for the need for haste was pressing, but I do remember her expression throughout – one of almost infinite horror. I am not always adept at deciphering human emotional signals, but I needed no assistance at that moment. We both knew that her life's work – the work, you might say, of the entire Imperium – had come close to being wiped out.

In the end, though, the worst did not transpire. The Emperor's project was not entirely lost. All that we had learned over those long centuries of recovery did not disappear, though the body of it was gravely damaged. I carried vials from the flames myself, feeling the pulse of life within them through my gauntlets.

When all was done, we were forced to withdraw. Many of the deeper caches were abandoned to the flames. The entire structure began to subside at last, and our remaining forces were ordered to the surface. I was the last to depart, along with Mal-cador. I recall running down the final corridor, the dust-plumes gathering at our heels, and reflecting that, for an old man, he could move fast when he wished to.

And that was the end of it. A great work, destroyed, with only the smallest fragments retained.

[Why are you telling me this?]

You asked me about it.

[I asked about leadership for the Thunder Legion.]

I had thought my intent was obvious. We were labouring to eliminate genetic instability. Had it succeeded, we would have created subjects with far greater control over their powers. They would have been the ones to whom the tasks of leadership could be delegated. There will be greater battlefields ahead, once this world is fully secured. Thousands of them.

[But it failed.]

It did.

[And the vials you retrieved were–]

It failed, High Lord. There are no new generals for the Impe-rial armies.

[Then, and I come to a difficult area, I have one more question.]

I know.

[There have been no reports of activity from the Thunder Legion for months. Silence, even in the High Council, where we used to be sent bulletins. Is their absence somehow related to this episode? Or has some security protocol changed that keeps their movements secret?]

I have answered your questions.

[You have. In greater detail than I could have hoped for. But not, so far, on the central matter. What happened on Mount Ararat, captain-general?]

You are out of time.

[I went there. I saw the remains. What happened to the Thunder Warriors?]

-- Transcript ends --

NINE

The air was already getting thin.

It had been cold for the entire journey, painfully so at the halts where the engines were allowed to gutter out to save fuel, but now the collapsing temperatures were becoming an issue. The transports were mostly old. Many of them had the Raptor Imperialis etched onto their sides, especially up in the vanguard where the really heavy armour was concentrated. Achilla wouldn't have known much about that, though – his place was firmly in the expendable bracket, back where the pre-Imperial personnel carriers spluttered and rocked to climb the dusty mountain paths. Everything smelled of heavy fuel oils, even when the wind blew hard, which it seemed to do all the time.

Achilla hung to the side of his unit's carrier and peered up ahead. As it had been for as long as he could remember, the land was rising steeply. Burned-out forests with black, broken sticks for trees, the legacy of some old apocalypse, had given way to a hardscrabble landscape of frozen rubble. The sky was grey-black, as heavy a build-up of thunderheads as he'd ever seen, and it had been sleeting for hours without let-up. The earth roads under them were steadily subsiding into a soup of pale, loose gravel, and even the convoy's halftracks were struggling to maintain speed.

The ultimate destination was hidden from view by a serried screen of towering cliff-faces, each one more immense than the last. The convoy would have to climb much further before the great terraformed plateau around the Palace would make things easier. For the moment, they were seeing the mountains much as they had existed for all of humanity's history – a bulwark against any kind of movement, impassable and magnificent. It was the Imperium's great triumph to tame this unimaginably huge massif, to lay roads across it, to fill its valleys and level its most daunting summits. Ironically, of course, that was also what offered the possibility of approach.

A 'crusade', the commanders had called it. Achilla didn't like that term. It felt too close to what he'd been told when fighting among the zealots of Unity. He didn't like to think too closely about the motivations for this at all, only that it was a chance to strike back at something that had already become complacent and authoritarian. There was always the chance that he was being used now by someone else, someone just as complacent and authoritarian, but what else was there to do, for such as he? Achilla had only ever been good at one thing, and at least this was a chance to demonstrate it one last time.

'Going to be a big one,' said Slak, standing next to him on the footplate, clinging to the transport's side one-handed.

'Aye,' said Achilla, glancing up at the gathering storm. The air, though thinned, already felt charged, as if by static. The sleet was cascading down the transport's flanks freely. 'It'll make this difficult.'

'For them, too.'

Slak was a big man, though all that old muscle was running to fat now. His beard was bedraggled in the downpour, and stuck in matted tufts across a riveted breast-plate. His thermal lance, strapped to his back, was covered in tarpaulin against the elements. Achilla thought it would have been wiser to keep it stowed in the crew-compartment, out of the weather, but Slak liked to have his weapon close at all times, and you didn't argue with Slak about some things.

After another two hours of hard slogging, passing the broken-down, weather-beaten wrecks of a dozen of their own trans-ports, the piebald army reached the final charted settlement before hitting the high plateau. Achilla didn't know the name of the place. It was a grim, grey kind of conurbation, all indus-trial complexes and refineries, belching columns of vapour into the high airs. There were no walls, no guard-towers, so the con-voy just smashed its way along the central transitway, burning across reservations and gouging huge trails in the ice-crusted mud. Some of the residents came to watch. Most seemed to carry on with whatever jobs they had, heads bowed in the storm. Why wouldn't they? They had no reason to think that this wasn't just another Imperial regiment making its way up to the plateau for regular exercises. The world was at peace, now. All the raiders were gone, scoured from existence by the Emperor and His civilising virtues.

'I came this way, once,' said Slak, looking grimly out at the ranks of manufactoria and smokestacks.

'Oh?' said Achilla, not greatly interested.

'Long time ago. Nothing here, then. Just the wind. A few goats. Now look at it.'

Achilla hawked up spittle and sent a gobbet sailing into the freezing rain. 'These places are everywhere now, brother. On the southern side of the range, there are many more. That's why we came this way.'

Slak wiped his visor, leaving a greasy smear across the armour-glass rim. 'It all changed too fast. That was the problem. You can't make people change too fast.'

Achilla didn't know about that. He squinted into the murk, and saw a big Arbites station in the distance with a scaffold-wrapped comms tower. Beyond it was another large structure – possibly a garrison. 'We should take that out,' he said, sourly.

'Why? He wants them to know we're coming.'

'I know. We should still take it out.'

Slak laughed – a scratching husk of a sound. 'Be patient,' he said. 'Plenty of that to come.'

Soon after that they were out on the far side, having rattled through the entire place without a shot being fired. The road got better, no doubt used as a transport corridor between the industrial feeder-city and its central nexus. The sleet got worse, drumming against the armour-plating, and after a while even Slak had enough, ducking down through the hatch and taking his chances with the stink of mercenary inside.

Achilla remained up top, grimacing against the wind's bite. The kilometres passed in an uncomfortable, joint-shaking procession. He quite liked the silence of it. Every so often, he'd activate his augmetic targeter, cycling up to the maximum setting and peering far ahead.

The sleet was turning to snow. The sky was deepening to an inky black, and lightning darted along the eastern horizon.

It was a long time before he saw it. There was one last, difficult climb, in which he thought the old engines would finally blow out, and then they dipped over the final rise and onto the emptiness of the artificial plains. The wind howled even more strongly up there, screaming across snow-blown terrain under the shadow of curdled skies. Fresh snow had been gathered in the eddies and was now being vomited up by the gales, reducing the visibility to almost nothing.

Achilla shivered. His bones ached badly. His knuckles, wrapped under layers of flaking synthleather, felt almost fused to the metal of the doorplate. Still he stayed up top, squeezing every millimetre of magnification from his augmetics. It felt important, somehow, to see it unfold from the start. He'd heard so many stories about this place, and some of them might even have been true.

In the end, he only got a glimpse – the clouds were lowering all the time, the blizzard was getting worse. It was enough, though, to give him a shiver of another kind. He saw the ramparts for a split second, sweeping like a frozen wave into the tormented sky. He saw the towers ranked up against one another, hundreds of them, most still with the grip of ironwork supports on them. He saw the northern gates, carved from the mountain and then surmounted by glinting gold and alabaster. The Raptor Imperialis was there in all its battered glory, picked out in black and red and gold, as well as the spectre of its famous profile.

Lion's Gate.

Was *He* there, this Emperor, somewhere beyond that high portal? Would that make a difference? His golden monsters would be, that was for certain, and no doubt other horrors of the New Age, but the architect Himself – that would be something.

Achilla finally gave in, clambering down from the vantage and hauling the access hatch over his head. The interior of the carrier smelled as bad as every one of them always did, but at least it was warmer than outside. His boots sploshed in the dark slush across the floor, and he staggered to a berth next to Slak.

'See anything?' Slak asked.

'The gate, for a moment.'

'What did you think?'

Achilla pondered that. He didn't know. Something about the

place had given him a strange feeling, as if the storms were a
warning. Then again, the ones that led this thing were used
to storms.

'It's a doorway,' he said, reaching for a protein-strip. 'They all
look the same, before they're kicked in.'

He took a bite, and started to chew.

'And, to be sure, it'll get kicked in,' he said.

By the time Kandawire got back to her chambers, the entire
complex was already fully mobilised. The security protocols had
been enacted an hour previously following her pulsed command, and once she hove into view the external hangar doors
were ringed with lines of lascannons and over-watched by airborne gunships. After landing she disembarked quickly and
hurried to the rendezvous point. Armina met her en route,
and the two went in haste towards the groundcar depots.

'He did it,' Kandawire said, her voice shaking.

'You had any doubt?' Armina asked, dryly.

'I did. I genuinely did.' Despite everything, she had a sick
feeling in her stomach. She had wanted to avoid this so very
much – anything would have done, any excuse or mitigation.

'He told you, then? As you hoped he would?'

Kandawire shot her a sour glance. 'He shut me down, just
like before.' She shook her head in exasperation. 'It was very
strange. He talks, more than I could ever have hoped for, and
then says nothing. In anyone else, I'd say some game is being
played, but he does not play games. He would not even know
how to play games.'

Armina looked at her with concern on her thin face. 'If what
you suspect is confirmed, you are vindicated, High Lord. Imagine what it would have taken, imagine what it would have
cost… to end all those–'

'I don't know how it happened, not in detail, but I looked

into his eyes when I asked the question, and there was nothing there. No evasion, no guilt. I do not think there is anything he would shrink from doing, if he believed it to be somehow in his interests.'

'His own interests, or his master's?'

'His own. That is the issue. Just consider why this was done, for a moment. Consider what he has already told us.'

All around them, bodies were in motion. Kandawire's regular guards emerged from the rampart levels, thirty of them in full battle-gear, and fell in behind and alongside them. Menials were running from their stations, given the order to secure the High Lords' several citadels and wondering just how to do it. Even now, more orders would be pumping out along the secure node-relays, activating protocols for the mobilisation of the standing security details. It was all unfolding exactly as it should do, and in normal times would have been a source of some comfort. Of course, such manoeuvrings were all more or less pointless, but only Kandawire understood precisely why.

'Signals from the convoys, yet?' she asked, reaching the groundcar level and smelling the promethium before the doors had even opened.

'Nothing,' Armina replied. 'It's the storm.'

'How ironic,' Kandawire said, activating the unlock cycle and summoning Ophar's locator-bead. 'You should get out now,' she voxed to him. Ahead of her, the great adamantium blast-screens began to grind open. 'As in, *now*.'

'*Giving me orders, kondedwa?*' came Ophar's amused voice back over the link. '*Fear not. We are used to running, both you and I.*'

'I'm not running this time. But you are. We'll speak when all this is over.'

Then they were through into the depot. Twelve groundcars were waiting for them, their big engines already revving in a chorus of growls. They were armour-plated, six-wheelers with chains on the tyres and smoke-darkened projectile weapons running down both flanks. On the far side of the depot, external doors were slowly rising, allowing hard flurries of snow and sleet to skip across the deck.

The designated bodyguards deployed to their vehicles, four to each. Three more waited for Kandawire to take the lead vehicle. Before ducking into the crew compartment, the High Lord turned to Armina.

'I'm so sorry,' she said.

Armina, for once, looked startled. 'For what?'

'Insisting on this. You never agreed to it, and it wasn't your fight.'

Armina gave her a look of mixed bafflement and disgust. 'It was your fight. I am your servant. That makes it mine.'

Kandawire smiled affectionately. 'You see – *that's* the attitude we have to stamp out here. Imagine the Imperium in hock to such slavishness. Imagine nobody questioning anything.'

'Which is why we do this.'

'Exactly. And I have one more task for you.' She reached into her robes, and withdrew a shielded recording device the size of a child's fist. 'It's ciphered, and linked to your blood-print. It's all there. Both recordings, plus the evidence from Ararat. I want it kept safe.'

Armina looked at it doubtfully. 'You are the High Lord,' she said.

'Don't be facile. There's a saying from my homeland – when the elephants fight, the grass gets trampled. We are the grass.'

'And what is an... elephant?'

Kandawire laughed. 'I've never been sure. But there's at least one of them in the Palace.' She became serious again. 'This must survive. We are unimportant, but this must survive. He will never be as unguarded again, after this. I still do not fully understand all I was told, but the record of it *must not be lost*.'

Armina finally took the device. 'Then you do not expect to return,' she said.

Kandawire shrugged. 'I've been written off before. Who knows? In the meantime, keep it safe. Keep yourself safe.'

Then she disappeared into the crew-bay of the groundcar, followed by her bodyguards. The clamshell doors cantilevered shut, and the smokestacks belched out black smoke. Armina withdrew, holding one hand over her mouth and using the other to stow the device into the scan-shielded compartment in her tunic. The engines built up to an overlapping roar, and she had to withdraw as the groundcars screeched across the rock-crete. In a hail of snow and squealing, the cavalcade revved out of the depot and into the storm, making the entire space shake.

As the last of them crossed the barrier, Armina saluted them.

'The brave, it has always been said, are preserved,' she breathed, before turning, hurriedly, to make for her own transport.

TEN

Valdor entered the arming chamber. A dozen attendant serfs were waiting for him, each bearing a piece of his armour. Some articles were supported by two or more pairs of hands, given the weight of the individual auramite segments, and all shone with a glassy, almost dazzling lustre.

In the earliest days of the long campaign, even the Legio Custodes had not worn this gold. They had made do with what could be provided by the fledgling state they had been created to protect, and their weapons and protection had been almost as crude as those they had fought against. Slowly, slowly, the artifice had increased. Techwrights and artisans were brought to the Sigillite's orbit and pressed into more strenuous service than they had known before. Old skills were recovered, new techniques devised. The new ceramic compounds used in protective war-plate were the greatest leap forward – stronger and more heat-resistant than their metallic counterparts, and capable of being tooled with incredible precision. Motive power could be coupled effectively to the machined units, giving the wearer precise control over the level of power assistance. Many warlords on Terra employed versions of so-called 'power armour', but none of them had access to anything like this.

So when Valdor looked at his armour now, he saw the way every component fitted perfectly against his flesh, the way every component slotted perfectly against the others. Every sinew-link, every fibre-bundle, every synapse-jack – they were all works of art, tailored to him alone and wearable by no other soul. Once donned, the division between armour and wearer was more a matter of semantics than anything else – for all practical purposes, they became one unit, a seamless amalgam of gene-bred muscle and lab-wrought nanotechnology.

At the start, even he had not fully understood the need for the ornate decoration that overlaid these symbiotic links. He would have gladly gone to war wearing the drabbest of unfinished plate, just so long as it allowed him to achieve his objectives with perfect fluency. The astrological decorations, the occult symbolism, the martial finery pulled from ancient Earth's cultural archetypes, those all came from the Emperor's dictate.

'It is not enough to conquer as others have conquered,' Malcador had told Valdor, right at the start, just after the agonies of ascension had started to fade. 'You are the heirs of our dreams. You are the bringer of the new age, and the warden of the old. You are the destroyer, but also the preserver.'

Over time, the lesson was learned. A Custodian became more than a warrior. He became a living symbol, a marker of the Emperor's mandate on Earth. The merest glimpse of embellished auramite was enough to quell rebellions or send enemy armies into panicked flight. Soon, the only individuals capable of even meeting the Custodians in battle were those made so insane from combat-stimms that they barely knew what they were being killed by.

Every warrior of the Order became obsessed with his armour. Over the decades, they studied every niche and crevice in it, learning the curve and sweep of each individual item. Jewels were reverently set in place, all of them standing in esoteric relation to the others. Names were carved on the inner arc of the breast-plates, forming long lines like binding rope around the beating heart within. The decoration no longer seemed superfluous; it became intrinsic. They were form and function, aesthetic and mechanic, mind and soul. The donning of it became ritualised. Pieces were moved about in the proper order, fixed with the same procedures and locked in place with the same cares and gestures.

Now, as the long-promised storm flayed the Palace exterior, Valdor felt the familiar clicks and flickers of his nerve-interfaces sliding into position. He felt the spark of his armour's soul kindle against his own, expanding his consciousness into a shadow-world of advance-perception and motion prediction. Potency flushed down his veins, augmenting the already prodigious strength fermenting there. It was alchemy, this process, neither pure engineering nor pure biomancy, but something uneasily mixed from both fountainheads.

If he had been capable of arrogance, he might have revelled in the results. As it was, he had not had a single arrogant thought since the dawn of his new life-state. He had never taken pleasure in his capability, nor his equipment, only a kind of blunt satisfaction when an obstacle was removed, or an order followed, or a threat despatched.

And yet, there were half-memories – dim ones, like snuffed candles – of the time before. He almost remembered what it was like to dream his own dreams, or to feel the hot spikes of jealousy, rage or avarice. They had become intellectual constructs, those emotions, but still they were far from unintelligible. In rare moments of introspection, he found himself wondering

how much he had lost in order to gain the powers he had, and
whether the bargain was one he would ever have made himself, given the choice.

Such thoughts did not last long. Every fibre of his being was
set against them. Within moments, the obsessions would crowd
in again, and he would attend to his fine armour, and attend
to the mastery of his superb weapons, and attend to the condition of his already superlative body. As he did so, the old
words would cycle through his mind, over and over, like a
mantra of one of the religions he himself had helped to scour
from existence.

*You are the bringer of the new age. You are the warden of the old.
You are the destroyer. You are the preserver.*

The last item was slotted into place, filament-drilled and
given a spike-test. The final serf withdrew, bowing respectfully.

Valdor, now encased in his killing-garb, flexed his arms, checking the response of the auramite second skin. The air around
him hummed with danger, the most potent expression of which
was the idea, now fizzing through his neural-links, that all this
made him invincible. It was a lie, a malignant falsehood, but
it nagged around the edges every time this battle-aegis was in
place and complete.

'There is surely such a thing as too much power,' he had
said to the Emperor, once. 'Over-concentration in a single soul
brings risks.'

'You do not yet know what you will be expected to face,' his
master had replied. 'Have patience. It will not always be barbarians and petty witches who die under your blade.'

The serfs exited silently, shifting back into the shadows. The
great Apollonian Spear, once carried in war by the Emperor
Himself and now borne solely by His champion, hung in a
silver-flecked suspensor miasma, ready to be grasped. Once Valdor's gauntlet closed on the grips, there would be no withdrawal

from what had to be done. He could still experience a morsel of regret, though – that response, for some reason, had never been excised from his emotional life.

'*Captain-general,*' came Samonas' voice in his cochlear bead.

'Proceed,' Valdor replied.

'*You asked for evidence. It awaits review over the grid whenever you wish.*'

'Summarise.'

'*Her forces have been supplied and are moving into position. They will be ready to strike within the hour.*'

'Understood. And so I think I know what you are about to ask me.'

'*I detained an operative working on the core sequencing programme. She knows very little, but it was enough. Her testimony is recorded, should you wish to review.*'

'I have full trust in your judgement. Tell me her name, though.'

'*Liora Harrad, technician Class Tertius.*'

Valdor inclined his chin fractionally, detected a minuscule imperfection in his helm's response time. To any other soul that would have been imperceptible. It would not impede his responses in any measurable way. It would still require remedial work, once all this was over.

'An Albian name,' he said, thoughtfully. 'With a heritage.' He stirred again. 'Then you have full sanction. Move now, ensure this is done swiftly.'

There was a pause over the link. '*We are few in number here. Will you join us, captain-general?*'

'No.' Valdor reached out, into the suspensor, and gripped the spear. 'There are multiple storms assailing us this night – you will have to extinguish this one yourself.'

He started to move, and the doors to the chamber hissed open. Cold air sighed across the glass-fine auramite, though it would get much colder before all was done.

'*By His will, then,*' Samonas said, preparing to make his own movement.

'By His will,' said Valdor, closing the link, and briefly wondering, in an abstract sense, just when there had, for him, been anything more than that.

Magister Novacs Ilaed walked through the doors to the Inner Control Nexus, adjusting his starched cream tabard as he went. The lumens were too bright down here, and the projector-beads flashed from the white plastek corridor walls quite uncomfortably. Everyone hated these overlit interiors, but that made no difference, for this was her domain, and the only opinion that carried any weight in here was Astarte's.

The Nexus itself was a strange construction – an elliptical bubble of steel and glass lodged amid this orthogonal half-city of rockcrete and masonry. Its walls were curved, its interiors shiny. Every surface was pristine, an effect safeguarded by the small armies of menials who shuffled through its innards every hour. It was always quiet in here, though the low hum of machinery never quite went away, and the air always smelled faintly of almonds.

He could just about hear the storm flying against the walls outside. The narrow viewports on either side of the corridor were already blurred with the impacts of whirling snow, and there was a steady thud-drum against the arched roofs. The very idea of that maelstrom made Ilaed shudder – he was from tropical climes by birth, a native of the chaotic hyper-conurbs of Hy-Brasil, and this forlorn place perched at the summit of the habitable biosphere had always repelled him. Still, you went where your passion led you, and after a long and furtive career in genetic engineering during the dark times, Ilaed had been led here, one of many scientists sucked up by the Emperor's voracious war machine, scooped into flyers and brought en masse to the laboratories and research stations of Unity's showpiece citadel.

Ilaed had been told that, one day, the climate here would not be quite so disagreeable. That would, of course, imply that the Emperor was capable of altering the atmosphere itself. After what he had seen since arriving, twenty years ago, Ilaed no longer doubted it.

He reached Astarte's sanctum. He felt a hot blush of a dermal scan, and a tingle across his innards as the chromosomal wash took effect. A glossy panel on the right-hand side of the doors glowed green, then the doors opened.

The interior matched its mistress' spartan personality. The chamber was circular, more than twenty metres across. Light played everywhere – from reflectors, refractors, crystal tubes and finely channelled watercourses. The floor was white, as was the roof, and matt-grey synthleather couches ringed an open foyer. The only outside windows ran in a narrow band bisecting the two hemispheres of roof and floor, though all were currently obscured with storm-fury. This place was high up, and the hurricane outside was becoming ever more violent.

Astarte was alone, just as she'd said she would be. As the doors slid closed behind him, Ilaed realised that there were no servants present either, which was unusual – she normally surrounded herself with her creations, all of them subtly improved or tinkered with in some way.

'Reporting as ordered, lord,' Ilaed said.

Astarte didn't turn to face him for a moment, and so he was staring at her back for an uncomfortable amount of time. Her floor-length shift was as white and sheer as everything else here. When caught at a certain angle, the material was dazzling, generating a faint halo around her, like the angels of old Terran myth. She was so, so thin, as slender as the Tower itself, a mere slip of substance amid a sea of diffuse light.

That made it all the more jarring when, as she turned to face him at last, he saw again the grey flesh of her hairless head, face sunken across prominent bones, wrinkled into desiccation. Amar Astarte was the greatest mortal genewright who had ever lived, save the one who had sponsored her, and could have easily given herself a new skin, and yet chose not to. More than that, though, was the decay she seemed to have encouraged, as if to make some kind of statement, although Ilaed had never understood what that might be.

'Were you followed?' she asked.

Ilaed found the question insulting. The internal transit routes from the Dungeon to the Nexus were as secure as any on the planet, and he was no amateur. 'Absolutely not,' he said.

Astarte nodded, and padded over to a small, round column. Hovering over the surface, trapped in a suspensor field, was a gently rotating crystal vial the length of a hand. She looked at it mournfully, ignoring Ilaed. The vial glittered in the web of light, exposing bubbles in the milky solution within.

'Even now, after all this time, I find myself captivated by the potential we hold in these little things,' she said, her soft voice as dry as her flaking scalp.

Ilaed readied himself. When she was in these kinds of moods, conversation was a chore to be endured. 'Quite so,' he said.

Her eyes narrowed, following the traced arc of the vial as it slowly swept around. 'Hundreds of thousands of them, each unique, each cultivated with such extreme care. And yet, we could reach out – I could reach out, myself, here – and just… snap it open. How long would it last, then? A few seconds? But let it mature… Then we are looking at eternity, I think.'

Ilaed waited for the rumination to die out.

'Constantin would have let them all burn, had I not been there. I wonder if he would have been happy to do it. Had he known then what he knows now, he might have lit the taper himself. But then he was given an order, and of course Constantin cannot disobey an order. None of his kind can. That is the weakness at the heart of this empire – no one is disobeying anything.'

'There must be discipline,' Ilaed ventured, carefully.

Astarte looked up at him. A wry half-smile darted across withered lips. 'Must there? To give us the space to do what we do. But then it becomes an end as well as a means.' She reached out a gloved finger and placed its tip into the suspensor, almost touching the vial. 'It should make us fearful, I think. All of this should make us very fearful.' The translucent field flexed and refracted around the fabric of the glove. 'The great balance. Power and control. A weapon, its user. The former must not be greater than the latter. I'm sure you agree, Novacs.'

If Ilaed had understood, he might well have agreed. As it was, he had very little idea what she was talking about. Probably best to retreat into platitudes. 'The programme is on schedule. I am told that results from the proving grounds are promis–'

'What did you wish for, when you started this?' she asked, removing her finger and turning to him at last. 'The genecraft, I mean. What did you intend your legacy to be? Were you entranced by the science of it? Or was it the coin you were able to gather?'

Ilaed hesitated. 'I– Well, I found I had an aptitude for it. And, back then, it had to be secret, and in the service of the wars, so–'

'This is all still in the service of the wars, magister,' Astarte said, gloomily. 'Things are more systematic, that is true. We have achieved more than I would have ever thought possible. They are ready. They are as perfect as we are ever likely to make them. Mass production will follow when they figure out how to achieve that, and after that no one will remember it, but we were the ones who made it all happen.'

'It was the Emperor's genius.'

'Very true. Not just His, though. Many minds have been involved in this from the start. There has been dispute, there has been divergence, and there has been treachery.'

'Treachery?'

'What did you wish to speak to me about, magister?'

Ilaed blinked. It was always so hard to keep up with what she wanted. Astarte was brilliant, her speech razor-rapid, but her mind was like an accelerator tube – zinging and rebounding with particles that went off in all directions.

'One of my staff is missing.'

Astarte smiled. 'How unfortunate. How many do you have?'

'One thousand, three hundred and forty.'

'And you keep a close eye on them all.'

'I try to. She is a technician, Liora Harrad.'

'Class Tertius.' Astarte walked away from the suspensor towards a white plastek cabinet.

'Yes. You know of her?'

Astarte depressed a bead on the cabinet's top, and a sealed tray slid noiselessly out. 'She is a fine worker. And has a fine mind. Finer, I should say, than her master's.'

Ilaed bristled, but stayed the course. 'She requested leave of absence for minor illness. Fatigue, she said. I gave her a period to recover herself, but she did not return to her station.'

Astarte delved into the tray absently, seeking something within. 'And so you, I suppose, made enquiries.'

'I did. She has been behaving unusually for some time, I found out. Several tracked visits to supply depots where she had no business to be. I discovered that she was seen heading towards a secure incoming facility just before she disappeared. After that, nothing. I have even begun to suspect that my investigation is being somehow frustrated from above.'

Astarte laughed. The sound was surprisingly girlish from such a withered mouth. 'Oh dear,' she said, retrieving what she was after and turning to face him again. 'I rather think you might be right, magister.'

Ilaed said nothing for a moment. He stared at the pulse-pistol in his mistress' hand. It was as sleek and white as everything else in this place, no doubt made specially for her. It looked wickedly deadly. 'Ah, may I–'

'I told you there was treachery in this Palace. You have already come to the same conclusion. You have come to believe that Liora Harrad may be implicated in it. Thus you have come to see me, to ensure that I am aware, and can now take action.'

Ilaed began to get worried. Something about her voice – always unsettling – had become positively chilling. 'Yes, but I–'

'Liora Harrad is an intelligent woman. She understands more about what has been happening here than you will ever do. No, I do not know what has happened to her yet. But yes, she is a traitor. I suspect that someone else has realised this too, and has decided to intervene. And that requires a response from me as well. For, you see, she was acting on my orders, and if we are to insist on using this dreary terminology, then that makes me a traitor, too.'

Ilaed was about to speak again, to try to get some sense out of it all, when Astarte fired. She was not a good shot, and the las-pulse tore through his shoulder, throwing him back across the shining floor panels. The wave of pain nearly made him pass out, and he curled up into a tight ball, his jaw locked in agony.

Astarte walked over to him calmly, still holding the pistol in front of her.

'Harrad may be the first casualty, but that matters little,' she said. 'Though she is, or possibly was, a hero.'

Ilaed tried to speak, but it was hard to make his muscles work. He watched Astarte loom over him, pale and shining, her shift glistening like samite. Ilaed managed to get his left hand to move, and tried – pathetically – to block the shot. But Astarte was closer now, and even she couldn't miss. The pulse lanced straight through his heart, killing him instantly.

Astarte watched his body for a moment longer. A black-red pool of blood slowly emerged from under him and expanded across the flawless plastek.

Then she turned, walking aimlessly back to the cabinet. Only two commands remained to be given. The first was to the team of servitors she had waiting outside – they would clean up the mess in just a few moments. The second was to her captain-at-arms, Jelice Bordamo of the Castellan Exemplars.

'It is done,' she voxed to Bordamo, putting the pistol away. 'No more deception can be effective from this point. Mobilise your troops and move on the Senatorum – we strike tonight.'

ELEVEN

The roads passed in a blur of noise, slurred movement and gathering anxiety. Whole sectors seemed to have fractured into a state of confusion, buffeted by both the ferocity of the storm and a gathering sense of inchoate fear. Things had never been quite settled here – there had always been an air of impermanence, of transience. Order had been imposed in the fullest sense by the promise of a better future, rather than the reality of life in the outer city – people were still poor, they were still hungry, and it didn't take much to scratch below the surface of that to reveal the fear beneath.

'It all degrades so fast,' Kandawire mused, looking idly through the condensation-misted viewport.

The groundcars had powered down the main transitways, looping between empty spires and teeming hab-blocks, kicking up sprays of snow and slithering about even on their chains. In the established centre, under the imperfect shadow of the mighty Senatorum Imperialis, things were more or less as they always had been, but once they got further out, into the sub-urban sprawl and semi-solid mass of shanty dwellings, the strictures became looser, and the inhabitants knew a little more about what was going on beyond those semi-complete walls.

The Arbites were out in force, though even their lumpen person-nel carriers slipped and blew gaskets in this foul gale. A handful of suppressor aircraft battled through the storm, searchlights piercing the gloom in fleeting sweeps. Some crowds were mill-ing uncertainly – many were heading further in, others seemed to be making for the perimeter sectors, their masked faces low-ered against the storm and swathed in environment wrapping.

It wasn't clear how they'd all picked up that something was happening. It was never clear how the great uneducated masses detected a scent of panic in the air. Presumably, some long-range sensor tower had gained a signal, then the transmis-sion had somehow got out over an unprotected line. Or maybe a menial blabbed, or was overheard, or had left their station and run out into the cold to blurt out what they were seeing.

Within hours, individuals were making their choices, or hav-ing choices made for them. Soldiers were roused from barracks and hurriedly mustered to the walls. Workers were sent from their shifts, told to stay home and keep the doors locked. Enforcers were given fresh ammo-packs and double rations, and kicked out onto patrol with orders to keep a lid on this situation – whatever it was exactly.

The closer the groundcars got to the gates, the worse it got. Within twenty minutes they would be closing on the main south-western approaches, no doubt clogged with conveyers and freight-haulers stuck out on the freezing asphalt due to the closing weather.

Kandawire looked away from the view in time to see the co-driver lean over from the cab. 'Signals ahead, High Lord,' he reported. 'Security details mobilising to cut off access.'

'Understood,' said Kandawire, quietly impressed that the place was being shut down so quickly. 'You have the coordinates for the secondary route.'

The co-driver nodded, and returned to his duties. A few seconds later, the convoy of groundcars swung heavily to the left, pushing from the main transitway and skidding down a narrow side alley. They left the overhead lumen-banks behind and were soon powering down unlit, slush-choked passages.

The speed of this, the sudden haste to get out, brought back the memories of all her earlier unplanned exoduses. Her entire life, it seemed sometimes, had been a pell-mell sequence of running from one place to another, trying to stay ahead of the rising tide of disorder. For the last few years, she had dared to hope that it might be over, and that her exalted position gave her some measure of immunity from instability. In truth, though, she had always known that turmoil would come again. The Emperor had brought some certainties to Terra, but the old pathologies lurked under the surface still, just waiting for their time to re-emerge.

She heard the chassis-mounted projectile guns load up – a soft clunk of ammo shunting into breeches – and then the eastern wall-sections became blurrily visible through the driving wind. There were fewer light-sources out here, just a jungle of semi-complete hab-units and the occasional warehouse, all looped with messy, snow-piled cabling.

'Scans complete, High Lord,' the co-driver confirmed, calmly. 'The exit route is guarded.'

'They're being very thorough,' Kandawire remarked. 'But I think we've got what we need to get out.'

'By your command.'

The groundcar picked up speed. The terrain opened up a little, as the hab-blocks fell back to reveal a wasteland of building materials and motionless lifter-scaffolds. Ahead of the wall itself, the ground fell away sharply, with the rockcrete giving way to unsealed, frozen mud. This whole area was little more than an aspiration – a planned industrial sector running right up against the inner curve of the eastern ramparts. At present it was just a big hole in the ground, with the foundations of future spires only semi-delved.

Building foundations so close to the walls meant that the walls themselves were temporarily undermined. The area had therefore been placed off-limits, and guards put on station to maintain a cordon over the vulnerable areas, but that was largely to restrict access from the general populace, and not designed to impede the passage of a dozen armoured personnel carriers with High Lord livery emblazoned across their shovel-prows.

Kandawire leaned forwards to catch a glimpse of the checkpoint coming up. City guards were racing to man a pair of gun-towers, and a heavy bar was being lowered over what passed for the road ahead. Las-fire pinged against the groundcars' flanks, flashing into the whirling night and making the vehicles rock.

'No casualties, if you can,' she voxed over the squad commlink. 'Just get us out cleanly.'

It had all been prepared for, and the groundcar squads knew their roles. The projectile cannons opened up, spewing lines of hard-rounds into the barricades ahead. The metal barriers smacked, twisted and blew apart under the assault, sending shards of plasteel spinning wildly into the storm. Under that concentrated barrage, the Palace security detail broke and ran, keeping low and slipping on the treacherous mud.

Seconds later, and the cars broke through, smashing through what remained of the security cordon and blasting down a long ramp towards the excavations. Mazes of scaffolding enveloped them, racing out of the dark, before the cars flew through the underpinnings of the walls themselves, bumping and yawing over the uneven terrain. Kandawire had the brief, unsettling impression of being buried alive under those tonnes and tonnes of rockcrete and metal, but then they were climbing again, revving up the slope on the other side and thundering up into the empty night.

She looked over her shoulder as they emerged, peering through the narrow rear viewer. The city lurched and swung, rocked by the jolting passage. It was dark, gauzed by the blizzard, smothered by the bruise-green clouds and the hammering winds. For all its imposing grandeur, it looked fragile then – a lofty citadel set against the elemental fury of ancient peaks. One day, presumably, the Emperor's vision would be complete and the place would be as forbidding as the mountains themselves, but for now, on this night, it looked precarious, clinging on, vulnerable. Even the walls were porous, in so many places, and there were as many informal gates as there were official ones. It couldn't last.

They drove on, keeping up speed, looping round towards the plateau and the many transitways that spidered out north and south and east and west.

'We are being challenged,' the co-driver said, interrupting her thoughts.

Kandawire activated the forward scanner, and saw the signal numbers mounting up ahead. Her first thought was that she must be mistaken – there could not possibly be so many. But then she remembered who she had been dealing with, and reprimanded herself for such lack of faith.

'Pull over when they ask it,' she said, retrieving the passcodes from her robes.

The groundcar slowed, then shuddered to a halt. The night air filled with moving lights – arc-lumens, the flare and flash of helm-mounted torches. Something metallic rapped on the armourglass, and Kandawire activated the lock-release. As the window hissed open, dirty flurries of snow blew into the cab and the temperature dropped to biting.

A closed helm with bottle-round eyepieces and a chunky rebreather unit loomed up out of the murk. Behind that one, the profiles of power-armoured troopers clustered, all training weapons at the viewport.

'You'll want to let us through,' Kandawire said, handing the lead soldier her bona fides – a fist-sized ident-holder with the seal of the Senatorum Imperialis holo-marked on the surface.

The trooper took the ident-holder and plugged it into his ver-ifier. A few clicks and clunks later, and a warrant screed beeped into existence on the micro-lens. He beckoned one of his squad, who mag-locked pass-emitters to the hoods of the groundcars.

'On the ridge, south-west,' the trooper rasped through his heavy vox-grille. 'Command group has erected the standards – you'll see them.'

From there, they drove more carefully. The space ahead of them was busy, and getting busier. Big troop carriers were draw-ing up on the ice and coming to a standstill. Heavy armour trundled past them, driving laboriously through the gathering drifts with smokestacks throttling. Infantry soldiers were eve-rywhere, marching in semi-regular columns, all clad in thick layers of environment armour. Some were ramshackle, as she'd have expected – mercenaries, soldiers of fortune, augmetic regi-ments. Centuries of warfare had left plenty of dregs to be hauled up when needed. A majority, though, were Imperial regulars, taken from regiments whose loyalty to the founding ideals had not yet been eroded by servitude. It had been hard to assem-ble so many of them without arousing suspicion – that had been the hardest task of all, and the one to take most pride in.

They were not challenged again. The convoy rattled and slid its way through the gathering multitudes, weaving a slender path between the heavy tracked vehicles. Over to the left, where the land began to slide back towards the level of the great plateau, mechanised walkers were clomping through the mire, each one the height of a small hab-unit. There were even a few grav-tanks in the mix, struggling to maintain loft in the swirling maelstrom, their repulsor plates whining.

The command group was impossible to miss. Standards had indeed been raised – dozens of them, all bearing the Raptor Imperialis in its various incarnations. Lesser sigils snapped and writhed around those images – a hundred battalions and squadrons, all of them drawn from the architects of Unity across the globe. The largest and most powerful vehicles were drawn up along the ridge's lip, including the rhomboid profiles of the great Monitors, with their composite armour shells and twin-linked lascannons. Flamers had been swept across the terrain, mushing the snow into a churn of bubbling filth, and portable lumen-stands flooded the area with a hard, white glow.

'Far enough,' ordered Kandawire, and the convoy ground to a halt.

She donned her environment suit – a hideous black ensemble of thermal protection gear – and then struggled to get out of the access hatch. The weather-gear made her look even stumpier than normal, and as she staggered out across the mire she realised what a ridiculous spectacle she presented, set against this army of seasoned killers.

Her bodyguard came with her, but amid such company even they looked diminished. A troupe of mech-soldiers saluted as she approached, and escorted them all further along the rise, past the standards and the idling Monitors and up to the highest point along the ridge.

She saw the warriors emerge through the night-blown snow, standing motionless against the dark. For a moment, she thought they were Custodians, though their stature was not quite the same, and their armour not of the same quality. Up closer, and you could see the great differences – the plate was cruder, heavier, more bronze than gold. Much of it was heavily damaged, and individual plates had been replaced with cruder hammered steel. They still wore their crimson plumes, though, and still donned their thick crimson cloaks, all of it sodden in the freezing deluge. They carried their old weapons, the ones that had once been used in the Unity propaganda vids. She remembered seeing the first cuts of those, years ago, and laughing at the absurdity of them. No one was laughing now. They looked as savage as she had ever seen them, bereft of their old chains of command and now fighting out of bitter, wounded pride. Every movement they made brought a snarl of badly maintained servos, and you could smell the stink of atrophying flesh even through the storm's lash. They did not have long, whatever the outcome here.

They said nothing to her. Some, she recognised, were already deep into their pre-combat mania, and were working hard to maintain control of their faculties. Others were merely morose, or fixated on what was to come. Danger hung over them like a fog, creeping out into the frigid night. They had always been designed to cause terror, and that capacity at least had not yet eroded.

She saw their master last, just as was appropriate. He wore the finest of what was left of the old armour – bronze so dark it might have been iron, lined with blood-red lacquer and covered in battle-honours. His helm was encrusted with heavy decoration, the vox-grille formed into a permanent grimace. He carried a broadsword in one gauntlet, a projectile gun in the other. A tabard, scaled like a fish's flanks, hung from his slabbed breast-plate, and his blunt greaves were scored with the lightning strikes of the Legio.

Valdor was taller, it was true, but there was something

absolutely brutal about the man before her – a kind of ampli-
fied viciousness that made her eyes sting.

'Lord Primarch Ushotan,' she said, respectfully. 'It is good to
finally meet you.'

The Thunder Warrior inclined his ridged helm. 'You, too,' he
said. His voice was horrific – a corroded scrape, dragged up
from strained vocal cords and strangled by a damaged vox-unit.
For all that, he was still just about in control, still just about
sane. 'Didn't know if you had the spine to see this through.
Pleased to have my faith confirmed.'

'I had to be sure,' Kandawire said, feeling as though she made
the same apology to everyone she met. 'I never wanted things
to come to this.'

'None of us did.'

'I wish to remind you – no more bloodshed than is needed.
No anarchy. We are restoring, not destroying.'

Ushotan came closer. His helm was frosted with ice, vented
from the outlets on his rebreather. She remembered how Valdor had described him, up in Maulland Sen at the extremity
of the world.

I thought he looked like the ghost of all murders.

'We never broke our oaths,' he growled. 'Why do you think
we'd do so now?'

It was hard not to be cowed by this one, and yet she had spent
her life standing up to warriors such as these. All these fighters, all these men, genhanced or otherwise, all they saw was a
specimen of physical weakness. And yet, here she was, standing her ground, giving the orders. That was progress.

'Then I take you at your word, primarch,' she said, firmly.
'Be true to your promise, and the city will be yours this night.'

Ophar had been convinced from the start. He had been the surest, when the evidence was thin and the circumstances unclear,

and remained the surest once the corroborating factors started to mount up. It had taken Uwoma longer to be persuaded, but then in so many ways it had always taken her longer than it should have done to make up her mind.

People thought of Kandawire as impulsive, brash and prickly. All those things were true, but only some of the time. Her rise up from such a lowly station to one of the high offices of Terra had made her sensitive to slights from those who had found the ascent to power easier, and that led to the occasional outburst of bruised pride. In truth, though, she was not much different from the girl who had immersed herself in learning all those many years ago, who had wanted to stay in her father's compound even as it became clear that the end had come. She took her time. Before acting, she wanted all the facts to be laid out before her.

So it had taken a long time for the High Lord to truly believe that the Imperium's boasts of civilian suzerainty were hollow, and that the Senatorum's legal apparatus was simply a flabby shell designed to mask the actions of its soldiers. It had taken her a long time to believe that the Emperor could be either deceived or cynical, and that much of the rhetoric of Unity had only ever been superficial.

Perhaps all the gold and splendour of this place had dazzled her. Ophar had never been deceived – he understood why the Custodians looked the way they did. If you concealed your killers in the armour of gods, then they would be worshipped even as they raised their blades. Ophar had lived through the darkest of times, witnessing atrocity from coast to mountain, and knew murderers when he saw them. It didn't matter what they wore, nor how politely they expressed themselves – Valdor's soldiers had been created to kill, and kill, and kill again. They had no other function. Emotion had been knocked out of them, replaced by a horrifying *sangfroid* that bordered on the mechanical. They were devils. They were products of an age of nightmares.

He could, perhaps, have tolerated that had Ararat never taken place. The Thunder Legion had been the figurehead of the grand crusade, the image of the Emperor's consolidated might. Children would dress in mock-ups of their heavy armour plate and pretend to take on gene-witches or mutant-walkers. Adults would donate their tithes to the Cataegis, sending the credit-notes bound in screeds of thanks and admiration. When the Emperor's armies were spoken of, it was the Thunder Warriors who were venerated.

That must have rankled, even with such a dry soul as Valdor. Perhaps that had been the motivation for it all – nothing more elevated than jealousy. Kandawire had thought the Legio Custodes above such concerns, and in that Ophar had to admit she was probably right. There were other possible motivations, though – the well-known issues with genetic stability, the furious battles for influence and prestige between the various Thunder Legions that weakened their unified voice, the naked desire for power.

If pressed, Ophar had always thought the latter was most likely. The planet was well on its way to being conquered. The entire globe was awash with fighting men and women, most of whose functions would soon be made obsolete by peace. There would never be room for two Legios – the Cataegis and the Custodes – and Valdor was ruthless enough to ensure that it was his own kind that endured.

Perhaps, if such inter-order matters had been pursued through the mechanisms of politics or diplomacy, that struggle would have been fair enough – it was not for the Provost Marshal to concern herself with who was in or out of favour with the Emperor in any given week, and the military orders had always been, in the strictest sense, beyond her purview.

Wholesale slaughter, though, was a different matter. Ophar had heard all the rumours, both those swirling around the corridors of the High Lords' citadels and those that wafted their way to his ears from his planetwide lattice of informants. To exterminate an entire branch of the Imperial armed forces in one savage manoeuvre, without reference to the High Council or any other civil authority, was not the action of an enlightened state. It was the action of a petty warlord, and placed the Imperium in the same bracket as the Priest-King's confederacy, the old tech-bandits of Afrik, and all the rest.

Perhaps the Emperor had sanctioned it, or perhaps He hadn't. Whatever the truth, a stand had to be taken. Valdor's ambition had to be checked, and moreover checked by the true power behind the Lex. As far as the High Lords were concerned, the Thunder Warriors had never been officially erased by statute, and thus they were still in the vanguard of enforcing the Emperor's peace. This was the entire basis of this endeavour, and the one thing that had finally persuaded Kandawire to act. All she had demanded after that was that they should be certain. In the last days, that had meant one thing only – Valdor had to confess.

That had always been an impossible aim. Ophar had spent long enough tracking the Custodians within the Palace, and following the trail of the imported weaponry, to understand that they were already preparing to hold on to what they had. They knew something was coming for them, and had been repositioning their strength for days, albeit in ways that often baffled him. Now, with the dice having been thrown and Ushotan's scraped-together army standing at the gates of the Palace, he needed to see for himself how they would react. A guilty man always gave himself away when faced with the instruments of judgement, and it would be no different here, even if they were somewhat more, and somewhat less, than 'men'.

So he retraced the paths he had taken over the past months, back to the western redoubt from where he could observe the preparations at the heart of the city. The roads were crowded with soldiers on the way up, all of them hurriedly summoned to the walls by panicked commanders. Ushotan had not worked especially hard to keep his approach secret, but he had moved quickly once given the order, and the Palace itself had become a complacent place, a haunt of those who believed that all wars were essentially over. Knowing what he did about the numbers involved, Ophar found it hard to believe that the standing defence could seriously hope to keep such an army out for long. The Custodians themselves were so few, so mystifyingly concerned with their duties down in the deep interior of the Senatorum rather than where he had expected them to be – manning the ramparts, maintaining that eternal watch for which they were so universally famed.

They would surely emerge now, given the wolves slavering at their doors. There would be no purpose in remaining underground, when the already porous walls were about to be overrun. They would have to come out. They would have to expose all those devices they had been carefully hoarding – no use in keeping it hidden now.

He reached his favourite location, the one where he had an uninterrupted view of the Senatorum hulk. He squatted down, arranging his awkward limbs against the frozen parapet and cycling up his carefully tuned augmetic reader. For a moment, all he got was the grey-white blur of flying snow, then the rangefinder started to latch on to solid volumes and gave him a false-colour schematic. He scanned out through the storm-profile, looking for the heat signatures of individual Custodians. For a long time all he got were hundreds of false-positives – readings from unenhanced troops moving throughout the maze of interconnected buildings.

An hour passed. Then another. He did not pick up a single reading. They were not coming out. That was insane. The last living Thunder Legion primarch was at the gates of the Palace, and the guardians of the Imperial city were not moving. Without them, there would be no fight at all – the whole thing would be over before the sun rose.

He cycled through the ident-channels on his augur, possessed now by the uneasy feeling that something, somewhere was wrong.

Even as he did so, the upper reaches of the Senatorum hulk rocked with explosions, a ripple of them running along the high parapet level. He saw bodies moving – not Custodians, but troopers in the dark blue livery of an Imperial Army regiment.

Half recognising the symbols, he ran a check against the augur's data-mine. They were Castellan Exemplars, and they were heading inwards, not outwards. More explosions burst out across the sleet-hit walls, cracking adamantium plates and blowing tiles from the covered walkways.

Ophar got to his feet, shivering under his environment cloak. He looked over his shoulder briefly, south towards the great archway of the Lion's Gate, already backlit vividly by searchlights whirling. Then he looked back at the Senatorum, barred now by the rising pall of smoke.

We have this wrong, he realised, sickening. *By the gods of old home, we have this all wrong.*

TWELVE

Captain Bordamo did not have a will of his own.

In the most trivial sense, this mattered little. He could lift his arm when he wished to. He could eat and drink. He could take his lasrifle apart and put it back together again. He could express controversial views in the barracks and consider how he would spend his month's wages when the credits hit his regimental account.

And yet, in a deeper sense, there was nothing. His entire life, his entire purpose, was slaved to a single principle. That principle had been implanted in him before he had even become a person, back when his entire existence was accounted for by a few cells floating in a soup of nutrients.

He was perfectly aware of this. All of the Exemplars were. The entire regiment was composed of men and women from the Imperium who had, from the moment of conception, been destined for its service. They all knew, now that they were adults, that this was the case. None of them minded. This, too, was a consequence of their unique introduction to the world.

If he had been of a more enquiring disposition, Captain
Bordamo might have been inclined to investigate the precise
circumstances of this peculiar body of fighting souls. He might
have looked into the records of the hundreds of small clinics,
scattered across a dozen independent provinces of many different Terran kingdoms. Some facilities had been within the
boundaries of the Imperium, some beyond its reach. All had
been totally secret. All were now destroyed. The only remnant
were his kindred – baseline humans, physically varied, with
only a marginal, subtle tinkering of their otherwise unremarkable genetic make-up to set them apart from the greater mass
of mongrel mankind.

In practical terms, the outcome of this was simple. All of
them had been drawn, one by one, by roads crooked and hard
to trace, to service in the recruiting offices in Newdelii and
Agraa and Saac, and thence to action within the regiment of
Castellan Exemplars proper. Thereafter, they were loyal, diligent
and competent. They were taught, in time, the circumstances
of their selection, in order that there might be no unpleasant
revelations later on. This never discomfited them.

Most importantly of all, they became aware of their supreme,
in-built allegiance to humanity. Not to the Emperor's version
of humanity, but the true version, taught by the Prophet. Every
time they saluted the Raptor Imperialis, they would say the
right words and present the outward appearance of rectitude,
but in truth every one of them would be internally transmut-
ing the vocalised 'For Him' to a silent 'For Her'.

For the Prophet was, it must be understood, in a very real
sense, their mother. She had moulded and cajoled their DNA
with all the skill and dexterity for which she was renowned
throughout the Imperium. No special abilities had been con-
ferred, beyond a generalised nimbus of good health and mental
acuteness, for they had been created to be a contingency, a

hedge against uncertain times. Once the Palace was founded and the walls began to rise, they naturally found themselves stationed in its many garrisons in ever greater numbers. Why should they not have been? They were good troops, stable, dependable. The Exemplars lived up to their name, and never gave cause for concern.

Until now. The Prophet had finally given them the order they had been waiting for their whole lives, and they swung into action without a second thought. Every Exemplar stationed within the Palace reached for his or her gun, checked the power pack and spare, adjusted their flak jacket and peaked helm, and unfussily left their station.

Bordamo himself headed down from the Nexus towards the main security portals to the Dungeon. He jogged, his lasgun held two-handed and primed to fire. As he went, sixteen of his unit joined him, running from their various stations and falling silently into position. He knew that all over the Palace, hundreds of others would be doing the same thing. He briefly imagined that mustering, as if seen from above by eyes that could somehow peer through the layers of rockcrete – tiny points of dark blue, coalescing and re-forming like some giant amorphous organism, an infection within the body that would soon reach the vital organs.

His unit reached an intersection and swung right, now making directly for the turbo-lifts down to the Dungeon itself. As they did so, a six-strong squad of Seneschals challenged them.

'Halt! State your–'

They were the only words their sergeant managed to get out before sixteen las-beams scythed cleanly through him and his troops. A spatter of blood and fried flesh, a thud and a bounce of limbs, and the Exemplars ran right through the mess, never breaking stride.

Bordamo heard the first of the charges going off, and felt the floor shudder underfoot. That meant the perimeter-breakers had launched their assault on the inner core. Everything depended on speed now – there were thousands of guards within the near-infinite warrens of the underground kingdom, and they would respond once they had worked out what was going on and who was behind it. Only while the Palace's many sentinels were still confused and reeling would this thing remain possible.

They piled into the turbo-lift and hit the drop control. The cage doors slammed closed and the unit fell down the shaft, rattling fast. Once at the next level down, they spilled out again and into a large muster-hall. The space was already filling with Exemplars, more than a hundred of them. The bloodied bodies of Seneschals lay in clumps, as well as greater numbers of menials. Bordamo's deputies, both lieutenants in regimental colours, were waiting as expected.

'Resistance neutralised three levels down,' reported the first of them, a woman with valorous service pins on her flak-armoured breast-plate. 'Comms disabled, suppression actions already underway.'

Bordamo nodded, and made his way to the next drop-shaft. A wounded Seneschal lifted his head from the floor, and Bordamo absently shot him through his broken helm. 'And the Prophet?'

'Moving into destiny.'

An alarm went off somewhere down below, swelling up the many pits and transit-tubes, followed by the whine and crack of more las-fire impacting.

'Then we have no time to lose.' He made for the third drop-cage, hanging precariously over the shaft on taut cables. The unit could carry six, and there were twelve more of the steel carcasses open and ready for the descent. Most of the remaining Exemplars did likewise, leaving only a few dozen to strap incendiaries to their waists and take up position at the chamber's various entrance portals.

Bordamo hit the cable-release, and the cage lurched from its shackles. As always, everyone inside staggered, waiting for the swinging deck to level out and the lowering chains to kick into their pay-out.

This time, though, something caught, and the cage dropped only a few metres before snagging on something and slamming into the shaft's inner wall. The lumens flickered, briefly illuminating the oil-soaked metal innards of the pit-edge. Bordamo looked up, towards the rectangle of uncertain light overhead, trying to gauge what had halted them.

It took a moment for his mind to register what his eyes told him.

'Bring it down,' he ordered, and every Exemplar in the cage shouldered their lasrifles, aiming upwards.

Hard white las-beams fizzed up the shaft, one after the other, sending bright light shooting up the inner walls. Volley after volley hit home, flashing and spinning as the concentrated spears impacted and refracted from their one massive target. Amid all that dazzling display, it became hard to pick out just what they were aiming at – a jumping, shifting mess of reflections and distortions – but they had already seen enough to know what was reeling them in.

A single soul, a lone warrior, clad in that hateful gold and pulling on the main support chain, hand over hand, hauling up the tonnes of steel cage with its six occupants like a fisherman spooling in a line. The las-fire barely made it falter – the beams scorched and bounced from that impenetrable hide, leaving long black lines but little else. Steadily, agonisingly, the golden helm drew closer, until the Exemplars were firing at point-blank range, their lasrifles locked in terror.

They were thrown to one side then the other, slammed violently against the cage's innards and yanked upwards. Bordamo's stomach lurched, and he suddenly felt weightless, his feet leaving the cage-floor and his lasrifle loosening in his hands. As his head smacked hard into one of the big iron bars, he saw a blur of gold close to his face, swiftly replaced by a whistling sound and the rip of hot air across his body.

The golden devil had thrown – *thrown* – the cage across the muster-hall, slinging it one-handed and sending it careening into a heavy buttress-pillar. The impact was sickening. Bordamo was cracked against the skidding bars, his armour doused in a hail of sparks.

The sliding cage spun to a halt, and he felt the hot slick of blood against his armour. His left arm was shot through with pain, his vision was cloudy, but he pushed himself around and tried to aim at what he knew was coming for him.

The cage was a mess, a ruined tangle of dented iron, draped with the heavy bodies of stunned and broken Exemplars. Bordamo had the slurred impression of the golden monster coming for him, loping across the ground between them like some vast machine-wolf. He opened fire again, more out of reflex than hope, but the next thing he knew a cold gauntlet had closed around his neck, crushing him back to the ground.

He looked up to see a mask of auramite, barely an arm's length from his own helm. He saw twin lenses, flaring red in the dark, and a web of astrological engravings amid the scorch-lines of the las-fire. He had never been so close to one before. At this range, the artistry was almost unbearably beautiful, and the stink of incense was overpowering.

'Amar Astarte,' came the voice of the mask – a deep, refined tone that gave away its owner's lack of exertion. 'Where is she?'

Out of the corner of his eye, Bordamo could see other Custodians, maybe two of them, slaughtering their way across the chamber, churning through the remainder of his troops with a cool, casual expertise. They moved astonishingly fast, dancing effortlessly around the panicked las-fire before crunching their blades into bone and flesh. Already one had launched himself down the drop-shaft – others would no doubt follow.

'Too late,' Bordamo rasped, feeling his neck muscles contract. 'She is... already in place.'

The Custodian hesitated for a moment, as if considering whether anything more could be gleaned. Then he squeezed – a short, decisive, inward throttle of armoured fingers. Bordamo never even felt the end, just a sudden cold rush, and then blackness.

Samonas stood up, unlocking his blade as he strode back towards the shafts.

'We waited too long,' he muttered to himself, breaking into a run. 'Always, we are too cautious.'

As he went, the shadow-world of tactical perception swayed and updated around him, a multilayered gauze of target-ghosts and shot-vectors. He could see the marked signals clustering and breaking, every one of them an Exemplar soldier moving across the bowels of the Senatorum and down towards the Dungeon's secret chambers. Whole levels were now on fire, blasted into slag by incendiaries and now all but impassable. The infiltrators had done their job well – sowing confusion, generating false targets, sending the Palace guardians rushing to stamp out a hundred different insurrections.

He felt reproach stir within him – a rare emotion, but one of the few he was still capable of experiencing. He had never understood why this had been allowed to fester. They had watched, guarded, observed, but never acted. He remembered Valdor's instruction, right at the start.

Find a weakness, a slip in resolve.

Commendable, perhaps, but dangerous. Now the fruits of that decision were ripening.

Samonas glimpse-analysed the movements running across his inner tactical display, the shifts, the pattern of the fighting. Future-states spiralled away from him like spectres, picked out across his cortical feed in a glowing filigree of false-light.

He reached the lip of the drop-shaft, now slung with broken cabling and the tumbling fragments of the central chain-pulley.

'To the repositories,' he voxed to his command group, pulling them all from their killing and directing them towards the lowest levels of the hidden kingdom. 'With all haste now – time is against us.'

Then he flung himself over the edge, plummeting fast, feeling the hot air whip up around him and make his cloak snap, before he caught one of the remaining chains to break his fall. The atmosphere heated rapidly, fuelled by the furnace kindled at the roots of the mountain. He looked down and saw flames surging up the shaft, red and angry. His brothers were doing the same as him, racing down towards the deepest catacombs, dropping like stones through the winding pits.

There was no going back now. The Order's lethargy had to be accounted for, even at the cost of such extravagant danger.

Samonas gauged the distance, unclenched his fists and plunged deeper down through the inferno.

Valdor did not hurry. He went on foot, travelling alone down from the Tower and into the maze of streets below. Buffets of grey snow smacked and slid from his armour as he went, running down the auramite in glistening rivulets.

The sky was now black and turgid, roiling and churning like a thick-stirred slick of bitumen. The howl of the gale never let up, but shot freezing spears through every exposed nook, whipping up filth and debris and hurling it against the reeling walls. Civilians caught out in the storm ran for cover where they could, slamming heavy portals behind them once they gained sanctuary. The many mobilised soldiers had no choice but to endure it, heading in bedraggled lines to their designated defence-points. Those mechanised transports still out of position laboured through the murk, their tracks spinning and their engines thudding.

Valdor paid them no attention, but made his way calmly down through the terraced urban levels towards his destination. The flurries of airborne filth gave him a kind of anonymity during the passage – in normal times, the populace would have been shrinking back from him in reverence and fear, or maybe even creeping towards his cloak-hem to dare indulgence. As it was, even his splendour was obscured, swaddling him in a whine of wind-tatters and allowing him to move unseen. It was almost as if the entire climatic spectacle had been orchestrated for that very purpose.

He, though, still saw everything clearly. His armour sensors were untroubled by even the wildest storms, and his augur-range was undiminished. As he neared the outskirts of the gigantic Lion's Gate fortifications, he ran his projected tactical gaze over the army gathered in the wasteland beyond, counting their strength and comparing it to predictions. The statistics, as ever with him, were within expected parameters – the renegades out in the open far outnumbered those shivering on the walls, and no doubt exceeded them in lethal capacity many times over. That such an army had been assembled at all was a significant achievement, and Valdor found himself impressed, once again, with High Lord Kandawire. It was not easy to keep major operations secret on Terra, with its shifting allegiances and fractured politics. She had done it, though, just as thoroughly as she had done everything else.

He reached the looming bastion fortress, just to the south of the massive gateway itself, its upper reaches hidden by the driving sleet but its heavy foundations a dark, glossy grey. He climbed the long stair that led towards the bastion's inner ramparts. Troops of a dozen different units were taking their final positions, hauling lascannons and battening down the slamming access hatches. As Valdor reached the final uncovered courtyard before the gate's main transit canyon, a senior officer in the colours of the fortress' 12th High Watch noticed him at last. Caught in the middle of his duties, the man performed a fractionally amusing double take, froze for a second, then raced over clumsily to salute.

'My lord!' he shouted through the flying hail. 'Thank the Emperor you're here!'

Valdor kept on walking. 'Continue preparations, commander,' he said. 'No enemy must pass the threshold.'

The man jogged to keep up with him. 'By your will!' he stammered. 'But... but if I... There are more out there than we can... Will you join...? Will the Custodians be...?'

'Maintain your positions,' Valdor said, his mind already moving on to what would come next. His tactical readout was crowded now. 'I will pass through the portal alone. It will be sealed behind me. None shall leave by it, none shall enter.'

The commander hesitated again. No doubt he was considering another query, perhaps even a protest, but nothing came over the comm. Commendably, after a few moments more of confusion, he recovered himself and raced off to enact the order.

By then Valdor was reaching the gate itself. When complete, the structure before him would be truly immense – a colossal archway of coal-black stone and adamantium bands, buttressed and reinforced and surmounted by gun-towers until it rose nearly to the level of the spire-tops beyond. Even now, in its semi-complete gestation, it was still a vast construction, its echoing innards exposed to the elements and resounding to the howl of the storm. Whole battalions of mechanised walkers were intended to be housed within these hangars, one day.

Far above him, ranks of empty cannon-chassis gaped outwards, ready to receive the internal mechanisms that would allow them to hurl ordnance halfway across the plateau beyond.

The place was being built for another age. No war machines yet existed that would remotely fit into its vast alcoves, and the entire Palace itself did not contain nearly enough troops to fill out the halls of this one bastion. In anticipation of future abundance, the interior now shuddered with emptiness. As Valdor made his progress towards the heavy shielded external doors, his footfalls resounded high into the yawning vaults above.

Ahead of him, great doors slowly swung open, sliding along grooved tracks five metres wide, gradually exposing the wilds beyond. The portal gaped, more than thirty metres high, and swiftly filled with the flotsam of the storm's wrath. Valdor walked out into it, alone. The night roared back at him. As he strode across the blasted tundra, the gates closed behind him, and the high walls of the Palace steadily fell into the snow clouds.

In the darkness ahead, ten thousand lumens glowed amid driving filth. The high ridge beyond the plateau was occupied for its entire length, clustered with infantry and heavy armour strung out in a long, ragged line. Valdor's augurs detected the ranges of myriad weaponry all primed to be loosed – some crude and ancient, much else capable of dealing out tremendous damage. Above all, he isolated the familiar profiles of those he had fought alongside for so many decades of conquest, as singular as fingerprints amid the rabble of mercenaries and unenhanced troopers around them.

By now, the only souls who truly mattered were making their way down from the high ground to meet him. They had formed an embassy of sorts – two dozen Thunder Warriors limping along in their old, chipped armour, plus a diminutive figure in an overstuffed climate suit.

And then there was Ushotan, of course, almost as resplend-ent now as he had been in the past. He had diminished very little, like a granite crag thrust out into a wearing sea, battered by erosion but still defiant. He alone still managed to walk without the twinge of visible pain. His dark gold plate still carried a mite of its old lustre, and the campaign sigils were still just about visible under all the dried bloodstains. The power armour gouted wisps of smoke from a boxy reactor-pack, and his creaking servos were audible even over the wind.

Valdor met them in the scouring emptiness between the two armies, his storm-wracked city behind him, the gathered hordes dead ahead. They stood immobile, all of them, and for a while the sleet roared emptily around them.

'Death will come for you, Ushotan, one way or another,' Valdor said at last. 'You do not need to seek it here.'

The Thunder Legion primarch laughed. It was a sour sound, made machine-hard by his failing augmetics. 'Oh, I do, Constantin. Of course I do. But this is arrogance, even by your standards. Where are your golden sword-slaves? Where are your guns?'

Ushotan was a head shorter than Valdor, though built more heavily. The captain-general seemed almost untouched by the storm, whereas the primarch appeared to be emerging out of its heart, battered by it, fuelled by its inchoate wrath. The remainder of the Thunder Warriors glowered in the slush-haze, their armour mechanisms clunking and hissing. They were ragtag automata of destruction, assembled from rust and held together only by their fierce hatreds.

'You have demands,' Valdor said, equable as ever.

Kandawire moved forwards, unsteady in the gale. 'You know what this is about,' she said, her voice cracking through its hard-pressed augmitter. 'Crimes against the state. The slaughter of loyal forces in order to keep your grip on the Imperial war machine. By the authority of my office, you must now relinquish command of this city and open the gates. You will be tried in fair and open court, your fate determined by the Emperor when He returns.'

Valdor nodded. 'I see,' he said. 'And you did not think to serve this... summons when we spoke last?'

'Would you have obeyed it?'

'Of course not.'

Ushotan laughed again. 'That's why *we're* here,' he growled. 'Every fighting soul with a grievance or a thirst for revenge, and there are a lot of those. You couldn't erase us all – not *quite perfect*. That must really kill you.'

Ice-spiked rain swilled across Valdor's golden helm, sluicing like tears down the ornate swashes. His weapon, the immense spear, remained deactivated and sullen in the gloom. 'The High Lord is acting only as she sees fit,' he said, speaking to Ushotan. 'But you. You have served with the Emperor Himself. You must see how futile this is.'

Ushotan shrugged, sending cascades of rusty run-off shedding from his dented pauldrons. 'More futile than dying from my bad blood? I don't think so. I'd like to go out seeing my blade sticking from your spine, Constantin. That would be a good way to go.'

'Only if you resist,' interjected Kandawire, warily.

'Yes, of course, only if you resist,' echoed Ushotan, sardonically. 'You can walk back in with us now, and we can finish this without a shot being fired. But I don't think you'll be doing that, will you?'

'You know I cannot.'

'Do not be a fool!' Kandawire blurted. 'The city is undermanned, your order is scattered by the war. Resistance now will only cause bloodshed.'

'With respect, High Lord, you brought the bloodshed. The deaths this night will be on your conscience.'

'Conscience,' muttered Ushotan, amused. 'So you can remember what it's like to have one of those, can you?'

'Stand aside, captain-general,' insisted Kandawire. 'Tell them to open the gates. Your trial will be in accordance with the Lex, and if you are innocent, then you have nothing to fear.'

'Innocent, guilty,' Valdor said, wearily. 'I did not think to hear such facile terms from a High Lord.' He rounded on Kandawire then, just a minute shift of stance, but the power in the gesture was briefly naked. 'We are the architects of the species' future. No crime could be judged as too heinous if it secured that, no virtue could be forgiven if it hindered it. The Lex is a tool for the control of the psychologically free. It is an expression of His will, and nothing more. You have been a fool to think it more than that. You could have served long and honourably as its protector, and now your fate is chained to theirs.'

Kandawire held her ground, just, but Ushotan's huge frame, undaunted, shook with laughter. 'Now then, be nice – she has a point. You're a lying, murdering bastard, and we were all supposed to be cracking down on them. You could give her what she wants, and you won't have to watch your city burn.'

'Walk away,' Valdor told him. 'This is the only chance you will ever have.'

'We both know that's not true.'

'I will take no pleasure in seeing you slain.'

'You take no pleasure in anything. That's because you're a ghoul.'

'But I will end you, Ushotan – here, if I have to.'

The primarch laughed out loud, throwing his cloak back and sweeping his arm out wide across the empty plateau. 'Alone?' he asked, incredulously. 'You'll take us all on, *alone*? By the gods, you become ever more insufferable.'

'You cannot make a stand here, captain-general,' added Kandawire, an edge of desperation in her voice now. 'Despite all you've tried, all the weapons you've bought, we know your numbers are too few. You told me yourself – there are no new armies. All that's left is you, standing here now. And that is not enough.'

For a moment, just in the space between breaths, Valdor said nothing. In that instant, he seemed indeed beaten, or maybe resigned, a sliver of pale gold thrust into the heart of the infinite, ink-dark night.

'You did not listen to me, High Lord,' he said, finally kindling his great spear. 'I told you there were no new generals.' A halo of silver-gold light leapt out from its disruptor, dazzling as forked lightning. 'But if you had heeded the lesson I gave you, then you would by now know the real truth – that there are *many* more armies, armies more deadly and more numerous than any created before.'

Ushotan moved to strike, his own blade spitting blood-red plasma, and yet something stayed his hand. Something stayed the hand of every Thunder Warrior. Amid the roar and thunder of the world's fury, something new could suddenly be detected, something familiar and yet unfamiliar, something horrifically dragged out of the past and yet even more horrifically indicative of the future. There was a whine, a grind of mechanics, a surge of something massive and coordinated out amid the sensor-baffling chaos of the maelstrom.

'You should feel honoured,' Valdor said, hefting the spear effortlessly into its killing position. 'You are present at their very first engagement.'

And out in the driving muck of the ice storm, where the snow and hail screamed and the frozen earth cracked, ten thousand helm-lenses suddenly ignited, then began to advance.

THIRTEEN

Her own people called her the Prophet. At times, she felt as if that title must always have been there, waiting and ready for activation within the Exemplars' memories, and yet in truth, like all things, it had had its genesis. She had coined the term herself as a minor and clandestine act of rebellion long before the true revolt had ever been conceived. Even at the start, He had been so prim about the old religious tropes, and it had amused her to think of herself as the antithesis of all they were building.

And then, for a very long time, it had been nothing more than that – just a minor gesture, something to act as contingency against an unknown future. She had never been sure that the Exemplars would ever be necessary, but it had been an intellectually satisfying exercise to create them, carving out a fief within a fief, all out of sight, just in case.

Then the slide had started. The decay, the familiar pattern of degradation. Perhaps it had begun even before that night in the vaults, when the universe had been shaken by power of such magnitude that it had been hard to sleep soundly ever again. Or maybe that had indeed been the turn in the road, when the hubris of it all had become too obvious to ignore and doubt had begun to worm its way within her carefully constructed world of accomplishment.

In the very beginning, though, there had been no concerns. He had plucked her from a life of brutal obscurity, just as He had done with so many others. Warfare on Terra had been gruellingly never-ending back then, when it was still possible to countenance the annihilation of the entire species within a generation. The only way to survive had been to make yourself indispensable to those with just a few more scraps of power. The most usual way of doing so was through physical strength. With her, it had been the mind – she had proved almost pre-ternaturally adept at mastering the crude, quasi-religious techniques of biological manipulation that still existed in the scattered techno-clades, helping to create augmented soldiery for assorted warlords in their filthy laboratoria. She had learned fast, absorbing lessons from instructors before they were killed on a whim, studying relentlessly by the light of grimy tallow candles, using every trick and technique to keep herself one step ahead of cull gangs, kidnap squads and jealous rivals.

The creatures she had helped create had been, without excep-tion, monsters. They had led pain-wracked lives, often expiring before even reaching the battlefield, dying on their slabs amid strangled screams as their overloaded organs burst. It had never been possible to get used to that, to think of it as normal or acceptable. She still heard the screams in her many nightmares, the things she had distorted in order to keep herself alive. By that stage she had known so much genecraft that she could have left herself unmarked forever, a pristine specimen amid a world of tumbling debauchery, but she never did. She stopped ageing within, but allowed the accumulated horror to linger on her external features, the visible price paid for her many desperate bargains.

And then He had arrived. He might have killed her just as He did so many others, but He chose not to. Instead she had been taken out of the wilds and brought within the first strongholds of the nascent Imperium. Through Him, her eyes were opened to a world of purer science, of knowledge being recovered at such breakneck speed that it had felt that nothing was impossible and everything was permitted. Promotion had been rapid. She had been given command of a cell within the programme, and then a whole laboratorium, and then finally inducted into the inner circle of initiates.

'Arduous, but essential,' Malcador had told her, showing her the facilities to be placed at her disposal. 'Nothing can be done without genecraft.'

And the Sigillite had been right. Things had slipped too far, and global conquest required soldiers altered at the genetic level. By the time she was brought into His confidence, the Legio Custodes was already in active service, but the secrets of their painstaking creation were kept tightly under wraps, and in any case they had never been destined for mass production. He had wanted her for something different – armies of a far greater size, built for rapid deployment, bulk-produced according to standard biological templates.

The first subjects were disasters, shambling creatures little better than the flesh-puppets they were intended to take on. The processes were subsequently honed under the privations of constant warfare, in clinics and laboratoria that were kept mobile lest they be discovered and destroyed. Some of the lore deployed was old and imperfectly understood; some of it was new and volatile. Throughout it all, He kept them all working punishingly hard, inspiring with a word or a gesture, refining their crude initial attempts when necessary, opening up new vistas of possibility, persuading, teaching.

She had often wondered, even then, how far their own work was really His, conducted indirectly through mental suggestion or inspiration. He knew so much more than any of them, and yet He could not be everywhere at once, and so they were necessary, His tools, His band of willing acolytes.

She flattered herself that some of the key insights had been hers. Having devoted so much of His intellect and energy towards perfection, she came to believe He struggled with the messier business of compromise, and thus lesser minds had their uses. There was never time for perfection, and so the Cataegis were always a compromise. They were the best that could have been created under such conditions, but nobody believed they were permanent.

That had always made her anguished, just as it had before. Under their ferocious advance, an entire world was slowly brought to heel, but there was still the old price to pay, of pain and physical corruption, only this time set against the loftier goal of recovered civilisation. So even as the Thunder Warriors reached their apogee of power and fame, their replacements were being planned. These were to be more stable, more enduring, more flexible and more disciplined. They would be created in greater numbers, manufactured in batches just like the standardised weapons that were by then pouring off Imperial production lines. Most importantly of all, they would be permanent.

'Your progeny, Astarte,' He had remarked once, in a rare moment of possible levity. 'Your legacy.'

That wasn't true. Not strictly. Everything emanated from Him ultimately, including this programme, but there had been times, times of weakness, when she had been driven into fatigue by the endless work, when she had given into that dangerous conceit, and thought of them, for a moment, as *hers*.

But then the day of destruction had come, when the vaults had been breached and the instigator subjects destroyed. They had been central, those twenty primal components, designed to keep the new Legions from suffering the instability of the old. Rather than a patchwork of many gene-templates, they had been there to provide a solid anchor, a means by which excess could be tethered, and now they were gone.

She remembered how it had felt. As she had run down those burning corridors, her long-bruised heart had finally broken. There were no tears, no screams, just a silent, crushing implosion within, angry and impotent. Every safeguard had been breached. Every wall they had put up had been demolished. The certainty she had allowed herself to give into, the exhilaration that now, this time, they had perfected the formula, was wrenched away.

Each night since then, the flocks of old nightmares had come back with greater force. Every morning she would wake, her sheets damp, her flaking skin shining with sweat. She had heard *words*, echoing in those forbidden vaults, words that no mortal should have been able to utter there, because they had only been spoken to her alone, back in those first flesh-labs where the first subjects had died.

It should have been stopped that night. She should have had the strength, then, to put an end to it. And yet, who among them had ever been strong enough to go up against Him? What arguments could possibly hold sway against the momentum created over so many decades? She could see it around her now as she hurried through the tunnels – the things that had been built here, the enormous and complex structures, all for a single purpose. They could not row back now. Their pride would not permit them, even if it meant condemning themselves to the mistakes of the past.

And thus her long preparations had proved their worth in

the end. The subtle mental imprints, the long cultivation of perfectly loyal subjects, the contingency she had kept in the shadows against a day she had never seriously thought would come to pass.

They were around her now, her secret and unsullied faithful, keeping her safe, ferrying what had to be ferried and escorting her deeper down. Their faces gave away no fear, even as the noises of pursuit rose in intensity – Valdor's attack dogs, released at last, closing fast with all their habitual prowess.

The captain-general, though, had never been an obstacle. Valdor was merely a sentinel, charged with observing while others acted. He had watched while the Cataegis were born. He had watched while their successors had been planned. Now all he could do was watch again while it unravelled. To watch, to wait – that was his weakness, one that could never be bred out, for it was stamped into his very essence.

One of the many secrets Astarte knew was Valdor's original name. She knew where he had been born, and what his parents had been before they had been killed. She knew why the Emperor had risked a huge amount to carry armies halfway across Terra to locate him, why the entire enterprise had almost come to nothing, and what had saved it. It was possible, though not certain, that Astarte knew more of Valdor's early life than he did himself. He was so incurious, that one – a mask of duty, a mere cipher for the Emperor's own will. Whenever they had met over the years, which had not been very often, the contrast between them had been painful – he, physically perfect, silent and possessed of almost complete self-assurance; she, withered by toil, gnawed by doubts. She had been told in confidence that Valdor admired her. In truth, she could not return the sentiment. If he was the pinnacle, the absolute summit of the genecrafter's art, then perhaps it would have been better never to have started.

She could do nothing about the Custodes. They had been a fact before she had arrived, and would be a fact long after she left. But the other creations – the other experiments and deviations – her hand had been on them all. Her marks were within them, her formulations boiled and twisted within their blood, and so further work remained possible.

Just like her, the Exemplars knew the importance of this work, the last and greatest deed of her illustrious career. If a thing could not be saved, if a sample had been corrupted beyond hope, then there was only one course of action. They trusted that. They trusted her.

For she was the Prophet. And this, at last, was her time.

FOURTEEN

Achilla saw it all unfold. Just before they got there, he'd been shivering on the ridge, cradling his electro-maul in an armoured glove and wanting very much to use it. He'd felt the wind prise at the collar of his armour, worming the cold deep against his leather-tough skin, and waited impatiently for the order to advance.

The tanks were all thrumming with power, like iron beasts coiled for the leap forwards. Contingents of infantry stretched as far as he could see on either side of him, fully prepped for battle and palpably itching to charge down the slope. They could all see the city, tantalisingly close now, a heap of half-complete defences that looked ready to be washed away by the maelstrom.

But they were held back. Their leashes were tugged tight, all for that lone, golden devil, walking out without so much as an escort to meet the dying master of their piebald, haphazard army.

Achilla found that contemptible. If he'd been in charge, he'd have already loosed the mortars, sent the tanks trundling down to the plain and ordered the infantry squads to fall in behind them. There were no negotiations to be had here. Here, talk was, as it was everywhere else, a pointless distraction from the real business.

The first sign of trouble had been his oculus-targeter twitching. Its range-expander had been playing up ever since they had entered the heart of the storm, so he'd pulled it back from maximum power. That malfunction in itself had been odd – the device was meant to be immune from atmospheric contamination – but his mind had been fixated on the agreeable slaughter about to happen, and so he'd not paid much attention.

Then it had started twitching madly. For a second, a ludicrous second, it looked as though there were a whole new storm of signals advancing out from the northern approaches to the gate, marching in serried formation under the lightning-sparked skirts of the thunderheads. Then the reading was gone, replaced by a scream of static, and he could only see that irritating gaggle of Thunder Warriors standing out in the open like beggars haggling over scraps with the Emperor's golden ambassador.

He shifted position, feeling his old limbs creak in the cold. Slak had his lance ready too, similarly burning to move.

'What're they waiting for?' Achilla muttered.

Slak stiffened. 'Damn,' the big man said, softly.

'What?'

'*Damn.*'

Achilla turned on him. 'What?'

Slak wasn't looking at him. Slak was peering out into the storm, his helm-visor making a strange whirring sound. He must have had some kind of augur-mechanism in there. He'd kept that quiet.

Achilla turned back to the battlefield and tried to adjust his own augmetics. For a moment, all he saw was the snow gusting and the iron-dark terrain, all of it glowering under the relentless bludgeon of the wind.

Then, in a sudden data-blurt of clarity, he saw what Slak had just seen.

'Damn,' he breathed.

The battle-signal finally flashed across his helm-visor. The tanks' engines gunned into life. The artillery opened up, and the infantry commanders roared out their orders to charge, and it felt like the entire ridge had suddenly dissolved into a sliding wave of movement and unfurled aggression that surged down the slope and out into the open.

Achilla went with it, breaking into the run that he'd been waiting for all along. Slak and the others tumbled along the incline after him, tripping and slipping on the ice and scree. The wind screamed in their ears, and the hard boom of discharging weaponry split the skies.

His heart thudded hard and fast, stirring his atrophied old body into uneasy action. He still didn't know exactly what he'd seen in that one sensor-glimpse, only that it had changed everything. They'd been promised that the city would be undermanned and poorly defended, left to fend for itself by a military command hell-bent on conquest in the global west. They'd been told that the only fighting would be at the gate itself, after which they'd have free rein among the populace. There would be no plunder, they had been instructed, no atrocity, but no one had really believed that dreary talk – once these things started, you could never really drag them back.

But this was something else – something new, disciplined, numerous, moving down from the north under the cover of the breaking storm. Achilla had never seen anything like it. He didn't even have a name for it. He was heading into it, all the same. The ground exploded around him, blasted apart by the furrowing drive of anti-infantry weapons. Tanks skidded on their tracks, hammered by an incoming wave of crackling energy beams. The slush boiled off, turning the frigid air into a steam-hell through which las-fire pinged and skipped in eye-burning spikes. The night began to glow.

'Secure the gate!' Achilla found himself shouting. Others were crying out the same thing, barked from a hundred different vox-emitters and helm-grilles. It was all too hurried, too disorganised – this was meant to have been a walkover.

Slak caught up with him, lumbering through a hissing miasma of condensation. His thermal lance was firing, bolt after bolt, all aimed ahead into the rolling steam-clouds.

'What. In. Hell?' Slak was muttering, outraged. 'Thunder Warriors? Where'd they find Thunder Warr–'

That was the last thing he ever said. A single explosive round smacked out of the murk and thunked into his chest, blasting open as it impacted on the steel plate. Slak, who was a big man wearing heavy armour, was hurled from his feet and sent cartwheeling backwards, his airborne trail marked by flecks of cordite and thrown blood.

Achilla fired blindly into the mists. The jag-rifle in his left hand kicked with every loosed shell, while the maul in his right snarled with paralysing electrical arcs.

'Come *on*, then!' he roared, running hard along with the rest. A heavy tracked carrier bounced past on the left-hand side, its turret-mounted guns pumping wildly. He could hear the screams of soldiers being cut down, but couldn't tell where it was happening. He'd lost sight of both Ushotan and that golden devil, and now everything was an ear-ringing crash of full-throated battle, slammed up-close in a pall of sensory overload.

Then three of them emerged, thirty metres off, bursting out from the driving sleet, their armour slick from it, firing in studied bursts from guns that looked like heavy grenade launchers. They weren't hurrying, but striding with a terrifying collective certainty, laying down impossibly accurate fire in precise volleys. Their armour was all-encompassing, a tight-knit collection of thick plate, riveted and embossed, clearly purpose-built for the wearer and emblazoned with what looked like regimental icons. It was hard to make out just what those were in the gloom and muzzle flare, but Achilla thought he caught something like a winged blade etched on a dark grey ground.

Achilla fired, dropping to one knee and emptying his rifle at the closest one. His hits shattered across the battle-armour in a scatter of flying sparks, but did little damage. Two of the warriors advanced after other targets, but the third, the one Achilla had struck, swivelled round and came after him.

For something so huge, it could move astonishingly fast, devouring the cratered terrain between the two of them in just a few loping strides. Achilla kept firing until the chamber clicked empty, hitting it with almost every shot but barely slowing it. The armour looked impervious to harm – a segmented carapace like some huge insectoid, surmounted with a plumed helm and a snarl-mask visage. The whole outfit growled, gouting smoke from an industrial shoulder-mounted power-unit and crackling at the joints with released static electricity.

Achilla threw his spent rifle to one side, thrust himself back to his feet and swung his maul. The electro-feeder flared, surrounding the hammerhead with a corona of bright white energy. It was a good weapon, one that had crunched its way through dozens of enemies in its time, but it bounced off this creature's hide with a violence that nearly broke Achilla's wrist.

The warrior smashed the hilt of his grenade-launcher into Achilla's face, dropping him back to the slush. Achilla's head snapped away, wrenching his neck muscles, and he tasted blood across his teeth. Somehow he was able to evade the next attack – a drop-stamp from the warrior's studded boot – and thrust the maul back up for a second attempt. He managed to drag it across some exposed cabling, causing the warrior to stumble, giving him a second's opportunity. Achilla swung hard, struggling up to his knees, going for the weakness.

This time, though, the warrior was alert to the danger. The maul was caught in a dun-grey gauntlet and held tight, fizzing away like a sprite caught in a specimen jar. Achilla tried to yank it back, but lost his grip on the hilt. Weaponless now, he looked up at the monster above him.

As Slak had noticed, just before they'd got him, this thing looked so much like a Thunder Warrior. Pared-down, maybe, less bulky, with the flamboyance of the old Cataegis armour trimmed away and replaced by level-sunk rivets and hammered-down edges. It was grimmer, more functional, as if it had just rolled off the production line of some manufactorum somewhere. It didn't fight like a Thunder Warrior either, and there was something about its movements – hesitant, just a fraction erratic – that gave away its rawness. This thing was learning. This thing was learning how to kill.

'I taught you something, at least,' Achilla grinned, watching the warrior hoist his grenade launcher up, hilt-first. There wasn't much space for regret, in his world – this was always how he'd planned to go out, after all. 'You'll watch your cabling next time.'

Then the gun slammed down, smashing through what remained of his helm, silencing him for good.

Samonas sped up, racing through the narrow corridors amid a shifting twilight of fire and shadow.

He felt his body being pushed for the first time in a mortal age, strained to its limits by the need for haste. He had outstripped even his brothers by then, propelled by urgent fear.

Not fear for himself, of course. Since ascending into his modified state he was incapable of that, but there were other, more insidious kinds of anxiety – of failure, of falling short, of missing something or someone critical. This emotion was nothing so base as a desire to protect reputation or standing, but a locked-tight mania for the security of the Emperor and the Imperium, an obsession that never relaxed its grip on his soul. Every waking moment was punctuated by the semi-conscious tremors of imperfection and dissatisfaction – of not doing well enough, of needing to improve, of needing to ratchet up the levels of extremity just a little higher.

In his more reflective moments, Samonas could appreciate the psychological role of this trait, implanted into him by careful hands during the excruciation of his second birth. He could understand that it drove all of his kind to excel in their narrow duties, to never rest, to punish themselves until the goal was accomplished. Everything about his essential make-up was orientated around this one quality. The irony of the Custodians was that, though they surpassed every other warrior on Terra by margins so huge they were almost incalculable, they alone were incapable of drawing satisfaction from their superiority.

There were no victories, only opportunities for further study. There were no conclusions, only avenues for more strenuous application. The Legio Custodes were swords that were forever honed, becoming sharper with every iteration until they aspired to cleave the very heavens themselves.

And so Samonas feared nothing for himself, nor for the standing of his order, but only for the danger now exposed in the heart of the Palace, the place he had been charged with keeping safe.

He reached the heart of the Dungeon and tore through it like wildfire, smashing aside every resistance mustered against him. The entire level was still teeming with Exemplars, all of whom had been put there to slow him, to frustrate him, to keep him from where he needed to be for just a few moments longer. None of them lasted more than seconds against his whirling Sentinel blade, but even those momentary impediments added up. In the worst sections, where they had manned heavy barricades and donned infantry shields, it had taken whole frustrating minutes to clear them out.

His armour was now covered in blood and criss-crossed with las-burns. The deeper he went, the more scant the lumen-cover became. In those gloomy reaches, his cloak in rags and his blade dripping with gore, he looked more like some revenant of a devil-plane than an anointed son of Unity.

More explosions went off, just as he reached the processor decks. Bodies were everywhere, their necks snapped and their workstations destroyed. Long ranks of examination tables had been set alight, and the overhead lifter-claws ripped from their rails. The level of destruction was extreme and diligent. It had been done not just to hamper the work of the technicians, but to prevent it being resuscitated.

The air shimmered with heat. Flames licked up from every shattered surface, exposing the facets of naked black rock. The copper tang of human blood was everywhere, spilled both from the bodies of the slain and the cracked culture vials.

The chamber had been made... hellish. That, again, was a word that had almost died, and yet here it was once more, sprouting into fresh and foul existence like a black-sapped weed.

He knew where he would find her. Every blood-soaked corpse marked out the path she had taken, distributed at intervals like macabre way-stones. He went down, and down, and down – past the points where not even senior technicians were granted regular access, to where the rock around him was hot to the touch and where the chisel-marks in the stone had, so they said, been carved by the hand of the Emperor Himself. The air became thick, hard to draw in, sluggish as bile.

A final door presented itself, lurching out of the gloom with its seals in place and its security bar lowered. Samonas slashed once, twice with his blade, carving flickering lines of molten metal and exploding the power-unit. He kicked, sending the heavy adamantium panel tumbling away, and was across the threshold and into a world of dark crimson ambience and the nerve-fraying hum of massive engines.

The vault was gigantic – a long, high, narrow shaft in the world's crust that led onwards into occlusion. It was barely ten metres wide, but extended ahead for many hundred, like the nave of some half-formed cathedral, buried under the mountains' roots and secure against any possible apocalypse on the surface.

The floor was undressed rockcrete, antiseptically clean but bare and unadorned. The roof was lost in shadow, far out of mortal eyesight. The walls on either side were glassy, shining like a field of stars amid a sullen red glow of bank lumens. Every square metre was marked by the same detail – row upon row of vials, all stacked with perfect precision and marked with identifier runes. At regular intervals the colossal racks were scored with larger sigils engraved in gold – a raptor, a lightning strike, a drop of blood surmounted by stylised wings, a wolf's head.

Samonas barely had time to take those in, though, for his quarry was sighted and ahead of him. Gangs of Exemplars were finalising their work – hauling crates on chain-lifts, rigging cables, connecting power packs. Even as he sprinted towards them, Samonas was calculating the optimal path of slaughter. There were dozens present, some already firing at him, others busy with their work.

He leapt, swinging his body around in a twist and hurling his blade's edge out wide. That stroke took out four in a single movement, lacerating through their armour without slowing. Then he was properly among them, in close, punching, kicking, thrusting, a tornado of movement. He jutted his gauntlet out, catching an Exemplar in the chest and cracking him back against the vial-racks, breaking his back. In the same moment, his blade punched through the stomach of another, lifting the victim from the ground before a flick of a wrist sent the flailing corpse bouncing three metres down the floor.

Then he saw her, Astarte, twenty metres further up along the shaft, perched high up on a rack-mounted access platform slung between the twin walls of glass. He whipped his sword up and loosed two shots from its hilt-mounted bolter, aimed perfectly, before leaping up to grasp a handhold on the nearside wall.

Astarte made no attempt to evade the shells, and they exploded harmlessly across a glittering ovoid barrier – a personal void shield, something beyond price, something even the greatest of the Emperor's servants would have struggled to acquire easily.

'Your presence here is pointless, Custodian,' she called out wearily, activating the access platform's motors. The flimsy structure began to shunt upwards, powered by an underslung battery of glowing suspensors. 'All is completed. All is done.'

Samonas clambered after the rising platform, using the shelves as a ladder, noticing just how extensive the net of cabling around them both was, and how many heavy clusters of incendiaries had already been installed in position. It would take hours to untangle it all, and no doubt it had been rigged to blow if tampered with. Every movement he made – every grip on a metal shelf with his gauntlet, every kick with his boot – smashed more glass vials, sending cascades of twinkling shards falling to the floor below.

'Remain where you are!' he warned, firing at the platform's suspensors in a bid to bring it down, only for more close-range void shields to extinguish the shell's explosion. 'The Emperor's Judgement is upon you!'

Astarte laughed sourly, still gaining height. Samonas saw that she was unarmed, save for something that looked like a remote detonator in one hand. He climbed faster.

'I really would not expect you to understand this,' Astarte told him, calmly. 'Go carefully – you are trampling on your usurpers.'

A shelf snapped, bent by his weight, and Samonas nearly lost his footing. He reached out with his one free hand, for a moment dangling precariously. 'Do not do this!' he called out again, feeling more shelves creak under his weight. 'This is your work. This is your honoured work.'

Astarte's face, unhidden behind any helm or protection, twisted into a grimace. 'True. Work I believed in.' Her voice was wracked with unfeigned pain. 'But it cannot be completed. It cannot be made perfect. We are making Thunder Warriors again. They will fail. There is sickness in their flesh, in all this flesh. They cannot but fail.'

Samonas started to climb again, going carefully, trying to ignore the way the shelves flexed and distorted under his bulk. More vials tumbled to the distant floor, smashing as they hit. Astarte was running out of room – soon she would be as high as the platform would take her.

'That is not your decision to make,' he warned, reaching a support pillar and seizing it.

'Ah, it is so very much my decision to make,' Astarte replied, bitterly. 'I created them. My knowledge is in them, mixed with all His chem-strands and gene-tangles. I worked so hard to cure them, but the originals are gone. Gone. You understand this? The whole project was *them*. We needed *them*. All we have left are the dregs, the by-blows to pull together and meld into something workable. It can't be done. You hear me, Custodian? It *can't be done*.'

Samonas felt another shelf crack, and flung himself across a column-gap towards a more stable section. The platform's ascent began to slow. They were both a long way up now. A fall would certainly kill her. It might even kill him.

'I care not,' he called out. 'This is the Emperor's domain. Unless He orders me otherwise, I will protect it.'

'Ha!' Astarte snorted. 'You have no idea what He plans. He thinks He's running out of time. You know that? He's terrified of it, so He's reaching out for anything that will keep the predator at bay for a little longer. He'll go to war with this poisoned army of flawed monsters, because He never listens. Least of all to me.'

The platform reached the upper levels, and its brakes began to squeeze the rails. Samonas scanned it for weakness, and saw a tiny potential gap where the runners met the chain-links. The void coverage would gape just a little there – less than a centimetre, but only fully when the platform was stationary.

'Surrender yourself,' he warned for a final time, gauging what would be needed. 'I will not permit harm to come to this place.'

'I cannot let them live,' Astarte said, almost pleadingly, reaching for the detonator's controls. It looked as though there were tears running down her cheeks. 'I know what they would do. They are my children, but I cannot let them live.'

'Stay your hand.'

'We were so close. Let that be history's verdict – we were *so close*.'

The platform shuddered to a halt. Samonas flung his sword, blade over hilt, at the gap. The aim was flawless, and the tip sheared through the narrow cleft, jamming fast amid the chains and gears. The void shields blew, exploding in sequence along the platform's length. Astarte disappeared behind a static-laced inferno, screaming incoherently, but by then Samonas was already racing up the last of the vial-shelves. He launched himself across the gap, his fingers clamping on to the reeling platform, his weight near-wrenching it from its rail-housings. He swung for a moment, suspended fifty metres up, before hauling himself onto the teetering surface.

Astarte was on her knees. The detonator had been knocked from her grasp and was skittering across the tilted metal-mesh floor. She scrambled after it.

Samonas was faster. Compensating effortlessly for the tilting deck, he pounced, crushing the metal box in his gauntlet before swinging back to face Astarte.

She was wounded – lines of blood ran freely down her ravaged face – and she seemed unable to get to her feet. Her robes were ripped, revealing an emaciated body within – all ribs and bones and grey-stretched skin.

She laughed grimly, struggling to get to her knees.

'Strike the warrior, fool,' she spat, extending her left arm shakily, 'never the weapon.'

Too late, Samonas saw the circuitry embedded in her forearm, skeined amid the flesh in a coil of glinting metal. The useless detonator, now crushed into scrap, had been the oldest trick in the lexicon.

He lunged at her, snapping his blade around to sever her arm at the elbow, but even he, even Samonas of the Legio Custodes, fastest and best of warriors, could do nothing at that range. Just as his blade bit deep, he saw the sparks of power run down the conduits in her arm, turning Astarte's withered body into a channel of destruction.

Down below, the receivers picked up the signal.

Down below, the incendiaries kicked into life.

Down below, booming like the tolling of great bells, the inferno was born that would scour the chamber and all its contents from existence forever.

FIFTEEN

It would soon be another victory, one more to add to the tally that stretched back through the decades. The deployment had been flawless, a silent advance under the sensor-killing aegis of both static-throwers and the storm's fury. And yet, as Valdor fought in his peerless, impeccable style, the air tasted of ashes on his lips.

Ushotan, true to his training, never retreated an inch. He roared into contact, broadsword leaking raw disruptor plasma, armour trailing dirty lines of filth, power-unit bursting with smog. The rest of the Thunder Warriors did the same, tearing into the interlopers, emptying their guns at them before swinging their crackling blades. Reinforcements from the ridge arrived swiftly, racing down the slope to engage, headed by the many tanks that ploughed and laboured in the dirt-drifts, filling the night with the coruscating fire of their linked beam-cannons.

It was valorous, as aggressive as anyone could have asked for. That was what the Emperor had made them to be, and they had never let Him down in that. They must have known, at some level, what Valdor knew – that this would be the end for them, just one of a few lingering, grubby last stands before their short epoch was snuffed out. Still, they fought with vigour, determined to exit the stage as they had entered it – the slavering hounds of Unity, unrestrained, their jaws flecked with both spittle and blood.

'What are these things, then, Constantin?' Ushotan called out, hacking one of them down and striding across his lightning-arced corpse. 'They fight like they're constipated. Just like you.'

Valdor knew what he meant. They were raw, these first ones – still bleeding from the last of their implants, their muscles chafing against the initial marks of power armour. Their minds were bruised and infantile, ravaged by imperfect psycho-conditioning, and their weapons had only recently been machine-spirit-locked to the counterpart systems in their tactical helms. There was so much that was rushed about them, so many points of potential failure, and yet they were going to win this, because, acting together, they were already terrifying.

'They are the future,' Valdor replied grimly, taking out a lurching Thunder Warrior with a one-two slice of the Apollonian Spear, leaving a wreckage of organs and metal plate in a smoking heap at his feet. 'The Angels of Death.'

He was getting closer to the primarch. Airbursts of munitions blew across them both, filming armour with embers, and the two armies grappled around them in every direction. The tanks that Ushotan had so painstakingly dragged up here were struggling, caught by the punishing altitude and the ability of these new troops to take them on unaided. Even as Valdor swung round to face the next foe, he glimpsed one of the Angels rip the turret from a Serpent troop carrier and fling frag-charges through the gaping hole. By the time combat was joined again, that machine was just another blackening ruin and its slayer was already racing towards his next target.

'Well,' said Ushotan, panting hard as he swung his thick blade around. 'I don't like them.'

Valdor found himself admiring that dry-as-bones humour. He had always admired that about the Thunder Warriors – the humanity hadn't been bled from them to turn them into what they were. They had never had their emotions etiolated, nor their dreams plucked from their minds and left to wither. He would have liked to agree with the sentiment – to reply with something that might make both of them laugh wryly together as warriors were supposed to do – but, as was usual, he couldn't think of anything suitable. All he had were the facts of the case, the artefacts of duty.

'I do not much like them, either,' Valdor admitted, punching his gauntlet through the helm-face of an Imperial Guardsman before rounding on an already-stricken Thunder Warrior. 'But they are here, nonetheless. You should, I think, have seen them coming.'

'Ha!' Ushotan snorted, driving his blade through a second Angel and flinging its twitching body aside. 'We always knew something was up. He never made us *stupid*. Or maybe He did. Stupid to have gone along with it for so long.'

He was staggering into range now, battering his way towards Valdor with his habitual blunt-force doggedness. For all that, the primarch had taken damage. These Angels weren't like the power-armoured prey he'd cut down so contemptuously before – each one had landed a blow before the end. Cumulatively, they would have got him eventually, like wolves dragging down a bear, not that Valdor would have allowed it to happen that way.

'You had no choice,' Valdor said, now fighting his way into the primarch's presence, spinning imperiously on his heel to despatch the last of his bodyguards. All around the two principals the fighting raged unchecked, though the remorseless march of the grey-clad Angels was now breaking the back of the enemy counter-advance. 'None of us did.'

'You almost sound like you regret that,' Ushotan said, lumbering right at him, his blade held in that distinctive, rigid, two-handed style. 'Don't tell me you're having second thoughts.'

Their weapons crashed together for the first time – sword-edge grating against spear tip – and the kinetic release flattened a dozen fighters in all directions. Then they were driving savagely into one another, slashing, parrying, hacking, testing.

'I regret nothing,' Valdor said, pushing the Thunder Warrior back with a single, spine-jarring thrust.

'Only because you can't remember how,' Ushotan laughed, pushing back hard. For all his decrepitude, all his battle-damage, he was still a furnace of energy, raging against the fading light. 'Still, I always wondered what it would be like to fight you.'

Valdor smashed a pauldron away, ripping the metal from its shackles and exposing blood-laced flesh. He followed up with a jab that would have taken the primarch's head off had he not jerked back at the last moment.

'Many people have wondered,' Valdor remarked, battering him back another few paces. 'So they tell me.'

Ushotan was spitting blood by then, his shoulders dropping. His bladework never let up, though, and he kept on pressing, kept on blocking. 'They're all dead now, I guess,' he spat, trying to shoot another grim smile.

'It comes for us all, in the end.'

'But not for you,' Ushotan said, hammering back, putting all his strength into a sudden push that checked the Apollonian Spear for a moment and held it locked in a snarling mesh of electric overflow. Their faces came close for the first time – a blank mask of pure gold and a brutish pig-iron helm-grille. 'I always knew you'd outlive us, because I saw what you did to all the others. These... *Angels* will fight for you now, but one day they'll realise the truth about you. They'll see you coming for them, too late to stop it. We're all dispensable, every one of us that He made for these wars. All but you.'

Valdor threw off the deadlock, hacked back at him, piling strength onto strength. He could feel abundance flowing through his sinews, fuelling him with a familiar cold martial perfection. Already he could perceive the end to this encounter, its possible outcomes narrowing swiftly now, pitilessly shrinking down to the singularity of another conquest. 'I am nothing,' he countered, finding that he uttered the words with more vehemence than he'd intended. 'An instrument, to be cast aside when its function is performed.'

'And what function is that? Do you even know? Or are you just playing along with this, hoping it becomes obvious later on?'

Valdor saw the gap then, the weary slip of lactic acid-heavy arms, and pounced, spinning the spear and lancing it dead-straight. Ushotan tried to parry, and almost got there, but the strike was just too atom-perfect, and the blazing spear point crashed on through the primarch's breast-plate, shoving him backwards.

Ushotan roared, grabbing the hilt of Valdor's weapon and trying to wrench himself free of it, but by now the disruptor charge was spilling across him, tearing up what remained of his battleplate and searing into the skin below. Valdor cast him down, using the spear's leverage to slam him to the snow-piled ground.

The impact was shuddering, sending a shock wave dancing across the terrain and snapping Ushotan's spine. Grey-clad Angels coolly advanced around them both, past the kill-site, driving the last of the primarch's ragtag army back towards the ridge, leaving burning vehicle-shells and freezing corpses in their wake.

Valdor extinguished his spear's disruptor, and knelt beside his victim. As he did so, he withdrew a long knife from his belt. When Ushotan saw that, he coughed out a final dry laugh.

'The mercy stroke, eh?' he rasped, his face transfixed with agony. Up close, the black veins of fermenting poisons were visible on his exposed skin. 'The last indignity. You always were a miserable bastard.'

Valdor placed the tip of the knife over Ushotan's heart. Fresh snow was falling around them, turned brown and flaky by burning promethium. 'I meant what I said, lord primarch,' he said. 'I take no pleasure in this. You were one of our finest commanders.'

'And these new toys of yours – who will lead them now? Will they have their own commanders?'

'No. Those ones are lost.'

'Ha. All the better for you, then. The High Lord was right – you can't bear rivals.'

'It was not my doing.'

'Sure it wasn't.' Ushotan spasmed, hacking up oily blood. 'You know, when we were at Maulland Sen, and I said I pitied you, I meant it. I'm not trying to goad you. I really do pity you.'

Valdor remained motionless for a moment, his hand on the grip of the knife.

'I *lived*, captain-general,' Ushotan rasped. 'It was short, and it was painful, but by the nine hells, I lived. I'd rather have it that way than yours – no joy, no hate, no fear. Unbreakable without growth, immortal without passion.'

As Valdor readied himself to apply downward pressure, he had a sudden vision of a far-off future-state, spun out of reality and into the cold halls of an undiscovered time, where the galaxy itself was darkened by strife and whole worlds were cast into flame, where wonders and madnesses had been unlocked and now screamed their way through the arch of reality, where the foundations of physics creaked beneath the ravening scuttle of nightmarish unreason, and he was still there, still unchanged, still cold and pure and steadfast and unable to feel anything but the ubiquitous press of unending responsibility.

'What is left for you, Constantin?' Ushotan breathed, blood bubbling up between his burned lips. 'What more can He take from you that He hasn't already?'

Valdor drew in a long breath, then plunged the knife in, ending the primarch's agony. For a moment he did nothing else, his head bowed, the storm exhausting itself around him and coating the land in a film of pale, drifting grey.

Then, slowly, he withdrew the blade.

'Nothing,' he said, very softly. 'Nothing at all.'

Samonas plummeted, leaping from the faltering platform and ploughing straight into the wall's collapsing structure. He skidded down through the rows of vials, churning them up and casting a glittering wave of glass into the upswelling flames.

For less than a second he remained poised just above the churning plasma, a speck of auramite speeding towards destruction. In that moment he caught a final glimpse of Astarte's body as it tumbled away into oblivion, the platform twisting like a wick in the flames, and then everything blew into a roiling world of heat and light.

Even encased in his superlative armour, the press of the inferno was colossal. His vision snapped out, replaced by a white dazzle-flare, and his tactical sensors disappeared into a soup of distortion. He could vaguely feel the disintegrating shelves as he tried to use them to slow his descent, gouging into the metal plates to make his headlong fall just a little less bone-shattering.

When he finally collided with the rockcrete floor it was like being smashed into by a runaway land-hauler – both his legs flared in agony, and he felt the bones splinter. Heavy metal shards thunked down around him, slamming like molten rain amid the melting, churning world of magma.

He had no fixed point of reference. All directions were blinding, shimmering with flame, thundering with the noise of impending implosion. He could only visualise what must have been happening all around him – the vials exploding, ejecting their priceless contents into the boiling flame-swill before even the glass fragments melted. Everything was poised on the indeterminate border between liquid and gas, and when he moved it felt as if he were swimming through the core of a star.

And yet, even then, in the midst of that nigh-infinite destruction, the old manias still wouldn't loose their grip.

Failure. This is failure.

Samonas dragged himself forwards, going on instinct, groping his way through the flames towards where he thought the portal must be. His earpieces rang with the roar of the inferno, blotting out his own strangled gasps of agony. He felt the impacts of debris on his back, and the skin-shredding heat getting in where his armour had been damaged.

And yet, somehow, he reached the threshold. He hauled himself over the edge just as the entire structure behind finally began to fall in on itself. Even over the thundering outrush of the flames, he heard the cracking of the vault's pillars, the toppling of its ancient retaining walls, the boom of rubble as it poured into the caldera created by Astarte's destructive vengeance.

He felt his pulse charging out of control, his consciousness wavering. Every movement was a fresh excruciation, a harrowing of his already mortified flesh.

Too slow.

His limbs were like lead. He tried to lift his arm again, and failed. Something heavy crunched on top of him, driving a rent in what remained of his armour, and he coughed blood into his mouthpiece.

All he could see during that time was Astarte's face – that strange mix of ruin and triumph, curdled into madness, setting off the annihilation of her life's work. That, of all of it, was the worst thing. He couldn't get the image out of his head, and had the sudden realisation that it was going to be the last thing he would ever see, and that was a bitter irony – a mortal's scorn, marking his inadequacy.

But he was wrong. With faltering awareness, his felt his broken wrists being grasped, and his body being dragged forwards. There was scarcely any let-up in the fury of the inferno, but through the rush and howl of flame he began to perceive dark outlines – armour-clad warriors, struggling against the backdraught, pulling him from danger.

By the time they reached the first of the secure chambers, he was beginning to recover some of his awareness. The pain was almost all-consuming, but some of that now came from his body fixing itself, cauterising the wounds and combating infection from the burns. He felt someone wrench his helm off, and found himself blinking and coughing and spitting up more blood.

He was in the Dungeon again, far enough up to escape the furnace but still surrounded by the evidence of destruction. The floor shook, and the stink of burning made the air acrid.

'He will live.'

Samonas heard the words through a blurry haze, and did not recognise the speaker. Only when a helmed face swam back into his field of vision did he see one of his own order standing over him. Of course, it had to have been one of his own order – no other soul would have been able to withstand the flames.

'Were any others in there with you?' came the question.

He knew what that meant – any other Custodians, any other warriors capable of being saved.

Samonas shook his head weakly. Sensation and control were coming back to him, vying with the anguish.

'The vaults...' he began, his charred tongue thick in his mouth.

'Destroyed,' came the reply, emotionlessly. 'Nothing recovered.'

Samonas let his head fall back, striking the stone heavily. That was that, then. The entire operation, all the preparation, for nothing. His watchfulness had been in vain, and an enemy had struck at the very heart of the Imperium, wiping out its greatest treasures.

'There will be a price, for this,' he found himself mumbling, even as consciousness began to slip away again. 'There is always a price.'

SIXTEEN

She had started running at once. Just a single look at those…
things had been enough. She had seen what the Thunder Warriors made of them too, the shock in their initial responses,
and knew immediately that they had all stumbled, blindly, into
a trap.

She had no idea how such an army could have been concealed. Thinking back, she should have listened to the warnings
her heart had been prompting for a long time. Valdor was no
fool. The Emperor, his master, was no fool. The vulnerability
of the Palace had always been an illusion, something placed
tantalisingly in front of them like bait. And, like the eager sim-
pletons they were, they had snatched at it.

Kandawire was not built for this kind of exertion. She fell
often, crashing to the frozen earth even as shells exploded
around her and showered her with gouts of ice and grit. Her
environment suit was a hindrance to any kind of rapid movement – it kept her warm enough to survive, but swaddled her
limbs in layers of movement-inhibiting insulation.

She fully expected to die in those first few moments of confusion. The air was so full of the lattice of las-beams and projectiles that it had seemed impossible for anything to emerge from its heart intact. She panicked, hyperventilating as she saw the hulls of entire tanks ripped apart and squads of soldiers mown down by explosive rounds. She never got close to making the ridge again – by the time she had got her bearings back and started to slip and stumble towards it, those terrible grey-clad warriors were already tearing Ushotan's army apart and advancing into all corners of the exposed terrain. It seemed inevitable that she would be taken down next, just one more casualty among the thousands.

Only slowly, with mounting disbelief, did she realise the truth. Valdor's warriors had plenty of opportunity to end her. After a number of miraculous near misses, she finally fell on her knees before one of them, knowing that there was no way he could pass up the chance.

'Do it, then!' she yelled at him, her fists balled in impotent rage. 'It's all you know how to do!'

The warrior glanced coolly at her. He was enormous, close to matching the Thunder Warriors in size. Whereas they were gloriously flamboyant – barbarian kings in bronze and crimson – he had a brutal, mechanistic look to him. All facial details were obscured. His armour was so dark as to be almost black, with only a few prominent markers – a single 'I' on the breast-plate, a winged sword emblem on the right shoulder-guard. It wasn't even clear to her that any living person remained inside that suit – the profile looked like some kind of automaton, bulked out into more-than-human dimensions and outfitted with outrageously powerful sidearms.

'Do your job!' she screamed, out of frustration more than anything else. She had gone up against the death-dealers, and failed.

The automaton looked at her for a moment longer, then turned away, contemptuously, stalking after other prey.

She watched it go, dumbfounded. After that, more of them emerged from the charcoal-flecked storm, all of them ignoring her and going after the retreating remnants of Ushotan's task force. With them, the warriors were pitiless, killing with a savage efficiency. Even to her unpractised eye, it was clear what differentiated these new creatures from the Cataegis troops – the latter were warlords, all of them, as gaudy and headstrong as they were lethal. These killers were line-troops – undifferentiated, but collectively devastating.

Amid all the ruin, she found herself at a loss for what to do next. The screams of the dying and the desperate revving of the few surviving great engines were still deafening, vying with the maelstrom's roar to disorientate her.

'Get up,' came a familiar voice from the darkness, one that immediately set her teeth on edge.

She turned to see Valdor walking towards her. For the first time ever in her experience, his gait was not absolutely perfect – it looked as though he was carrying a slight limp, and the aurora around his spear tip was dimmed.

She remained where she was. 'You called your dogs off,' she said, accusingly.

'You were a High Lord,' Valdor said, as if that explained everything.

'Were?'

Valdor didn't dignify that with an explanation. 'You should go. You can still make a life for yourself, Uwoma Kandawire. Take the opportunity.'

She looked hard at him, trying to work out whether any of this was true. 'So it was a deception,' she said, accusingly. 'From the start. You were toying with me.'

'No, it was not.' As Valdor spoke, more of his dark grey

warriors fanned out from the smog-drifts, ready to pile more pain onto those enemies still on their feet. They were utterly remorseless, a grinding wave of metronomic destruction. 'You could have chosen to trust.'

Kandawire laughed, watching the ranks of warriors trudge past her. 'But I wasn't wrong, was I?' she said, dryly. 'This is the future. The Senatorum, the Lex, it's all a front. *These* are the faces of the Imperium now.'

'Conquest remains.'

'Where? The globe is all but in the Emperor's hand.'

Valdor drew closer. As he did so, Kandawire saw the damage he'd taken – the smashed jewels and dented auramite. 'There is more to the Emperor's ambition than Terra. This is just the start – already the ships are being built that will carry this army into the stars.'

She started. 'Is that…? Why were we not–'

'Come, now. Did you really think that the Emperor was still fighting warlords?' He leaned heavily on his spear. 'Luna is next. There are gene-scientists there, ones who can turn these thousands into hundreds of thousands. That is the task now, the one that must not fail. In future years, perhaps we will be able to indulge debates over the niceties of the law, but for now, and for all days I can clearly foresee, the task is survival. If that requires a few gentle myths – of choice, of determination – then so be it.'

Kandawire took that in. 'You can tell yourself that,' she said, doggedly. 'It may even seem right to you. But a myth will spin out of control. You let these things run loose now, you will not be able to rein them in later. I believed in Unity.'

'You still should.'

'But what *is* it, then? How are you different from all the others, except in power?'

At that, Valdor slowly reached up, activated his helm-seals, and pulled the auramite mask from his face. He looked at Kandawire with sombre eyes, letting the sleet run down his face. 'Because we are a necessity,' he said, grimly. 'We stand between ignorance and annihilation. To prevent the latter, we enforce the former. It is a bitter draught, and one you have been schooled to hate, but it must be swallowed.'

Kandawire looked up at him, defiantly. 'I will not believe that,' she said.

'I admire you for your persistence.'

'What happened on Mount Ararat?'

'What good can knowing that do now?'

'I want to hear it from your lips, just once. The truth.'

Valdor smiled coldly. 'For truth to be worth anything, it must be preserved. Within a lifetime, no one will even know the name Ushotan, even though he was greater than most of those who will take the credit for building this Imperium. It matters not what is done, by who, to whom, unless it is remembered. So I can give you nothing here, High Lord, nothing of any worth, for what you ask for is destined to be forgotten.'

'You are a coward.'

'Believe that, if it pleases you.'

Kandawire shook her head in disgust. Her shoulders slumped. A great weariness descended on her, and for the first time since leaving her quarters in the Palace, she felt the cold. 'Arguing with you is like arguing with a stone,' she muttered.

'Go from here. You will not be harmed. There may be a fate for you that I cannot see, and it would be a waste to extinguish it.'

Kandawire looked up at him, feeling old and useless. 'Why bother? Why not finish what you started?'

Valdor drew in a weary breath, and extended his hand to help her up. 'You were right about very much. But not about me. I desire nothing, power least of all, and certainly not vengeance.'

Kandawire hesitated, then took his hand.

'I wondered why you came back to the Palace,' she said. 'Alone, when the Emperor was still far away. At the time, it seemed strange.'

'He cannot always be with us,' said Valdor.

'And you, captain-general?' she asked. 'Can you always be with us?'

Valdor let go of her hand. The storm was beginning to blow itself out, exposing the rain-soaked walls of the Palace in the distance. Smoke was rising over the summit of the Senatorum Imperialis, staining the turbulent skies above. The structure, for all its novelty, seemed strangely old then, as if carrying the weight of countless years before it had even been completed.

'I expect so,' he said. 'In truth, I do not really know where else I would go.'

SEVENTEEN

The orbital lander burned its way through the clouds, surrounding itself with a gusting corona of re-entry. By the time it broke into the open its flanks were blackened and its retros whining on full power. It reduced speed, banking heavily to assume a priority approach vector, and then came down over the Palace's northern spire-zone. Soon it was hovering above a wide landing platform, part of the growing structural embryo that would one day rear many hundreds of storeys up into the air and be crowned with racks of battle cruiser-class macrocannons.

The lander kicked out a skirt of steam. Once touched-down, its stabiliser legs extended, the engines vented, and the shimmering heat-haze over its sloped sides gradually dissipated. An access hatch cracked open, and four blank-masked guards descended through the steam, each one wearing dark red robes and carrying a barbed power spear.

Finally, the main access ramp hissed open, spilling a rich yellow light across the slush-heaped apron. A lone figure – an old man – shuffled down to ground level, clutching at a long wooden staff as he hobbled. The cowl of his robes was thrown back, exposing a raptor-scrawny head.

All present on the stage bowed immediately – the guards, the port sentinels, the menials who had rushed to service the lander's fuel lines, the protocol and customs officials hovering on the edge of the platform with their auto-quills and data-slates.

All but one, who bowed to no one but the Emperor.

'My lord Malcador,' Valdor said.

'Captain-general,' the Sigillite replied, smiling warmly. He came up to Valdor and placed a bony hand on his gauntlet. 'It is good to see you. Though, from the air–'

'The damage, yes,' said Valdor, withdrawing the gauntlet and ushering Malcador towards an open doorway surmounted with a gilt allegory of Unity – an idealised man and woman overshadowed by a benevolent angelic protector. 'We shall speak of it privately.'

The two of them went inside, at first shadowed by the robed guards, then, once within the snaking corridors of the immense Palace interior, left alone. They ascended through silent and deserted rooms, climbing a twisting well of marble stairways before finally emerging into a high gallery lined with plundered statuary. The winter light, uncertain still due to the storm clouds piled up in the west, bled the colour out of the fine tapestries. Through the tall windows, the far peaks could be clearly made out – a wide circlet of stone, glowering under turbulent shadow.

'I am pleased to be back,' Malcador said, walking over to a polished ahlwood cabinet and taking a crystal pitcher of water. He poured himself a glass, offered one to Valdor, then took a sip. 'Luna really is not how I remembered it. There is a horror there still, just as there was in so many places here. The Selenar have made themselves mad, I think.'

Valdor nodded. 'Did they receive you in person?'

'We are not there yet. Emissaries will be required for the next stage.'

'It will not be enough.'

'No, I reckon not. Which is why I come back now – how did the Legion perform?'

Valdor's expression was hard to read. 'Well enough,' he said. 'There are weaknesses, of course, but they will do better next time. Recruitment and training remain... taxing.'

'Then we must redouble our efforts,' Malcador said. 'Having seen their forces, we will need more than one detachment. Three, I think, should do it.'

'We do not yet have three.'

'Then we must work harder.' Malcador put the glass down and padded along the gallery, his soft shoes sinking into the carpet as he went. 'Were there Cataegis in the rebel forces that reached here?'

'A few,' said Valdor, walking alongside him.

'So they cling on.' Malcador pursed his dry lips. 'It will be harder to like their replacements, I fear. Still, we are not making them for companionship.' He reached a life-size replica of an ancient Graeco-Roman discus thrower, rendered in molecule-perfect facsimile in imperishable stone. 'Always, He insists on this haste. He wants us to take the gene-cults *now*, construct the fleet *now*, bring the Legions up to full combat readiness *now*. It is no good trying to tell Him how difficult such things are, for He only sees the objective, not the trajectory. That could get us into trouble, one day.'

'High Lord Kandawire was removed from office,' Valdor said.

Malcador raised an eyebrow. 'As in... permanently?'

'She will not be returning.'

'Ah. A shame. I liked her.'

'As did I.'

Malcador smiled – a mix of wry amusement and almost-affection. 'Really, Constantin? I didn't think you liked any-body.' He glanced back out of the window, to where the sun was creeping in broken patches across the far mountainscape. 'We shall need a new Provost Marshal. I'll give it some thought. But, now, I am forgetting myself – the damage to the Senato-rum, tell me all.'

Valdor's expression never flickered. 'Astarte was given every chance. I held back, right until the last. She could have changed course, had she wished to. If I am honest, I still find the con-cept difficult to process.'

'As you should,' said Malcador. 'For you, treachery is merely an abstract. If it had been anyone else, Astarte would never have been so indulged, but then He always regarded her highly. What of the repositories?'

'Destroyed. The vault was scoured, the levels above and below sealed off.'

'Good,' said Malcador, and started to walk again. His move-ments were superficially stiff with age, but under the surface retained a certain brusque vigour. 'News of that will spread. The many eyes watching us will relax their gaze, for just a while. A high price to pay, for such brief respite, but there will be com-pensations. I shall tell Him the Dungeon may be repurposed now – He will wish to install the Gate foundation matrix as soon as possible.'

'I did not enjoy concealing the truth from my own kind,' Val-dor said, an element of reproach in his voice for the first time. 'In the past, the lies were always left to your people.'

Malcador laughed. 'You'll have to get used to it – more will be necessary.' His crooked smile slowly faded. 'If but a hint of it had got out, if any soul outside our circle of steel knew that we had taken copies and lifted them to Luna already, then the remaining caches would have been placed in genuine peril.

It had to look real. And, as you say, Astarte acted on her own volition – she could have pulled back.'

'But her name remains on the project documents?'

'As far as I know. A mild irony – He seems to enjoy those.' Malcador reached the far end of the gallery, where the windows gave out and the panelling darkened under the soft glow of recessed lumens, and his voice lowered. 'But there is one further thing, something genuinely unexpected. He now believes that the Legion primarchs may not have been annihilated after all. He cast His mind upon the ether, and found echoes there. He told me He thinks they may be recovered.'

Valdor frowned. 'It cannot be. I was there. The birthing-tanks were destroyed. There was nothing–'

'–left to see. Just like in our repositories. But perhaps they were not ended. Perhaps they were scattered.'

'Not possible.'

'With this enemy, all things are possible.'

'But, if they had them in their power, why not destroy them?'

'Because they couldn't? Even to reach into that chamber must have tested them beyond endurance. Or, perhaps, they acted for some other reason, constrained by rules of their own. They enjoy games, it is said.'

Valdor held Malcador's gaze for a long time. 'There were no new generals,' he murmured to himself.

'You seem almost disappointed.'

'Of course not.'

'Come, my friend. This is *good news*. The Crusade would be immensely speeded, were we to recover what was lost that night. Imagine it – the Legions reunited with their primogenitors, just as was always intended.'

Valdor said nothing for a while, though his brow remained furrowed. When he finally replied, his voice was thoughtful. 'I remember when I carried those vials from the flames,' he said. 'I remember feeling the life flicker within the glass. And after that, I remember seeing the first of them emerge from the amniotic units, glistening like infants. And then, later, I watched them increase in number, be given their weapons and trained to use them. I saw all these things, and I said nothing. And yet, Astarte, who knew them best of all, believed them so dangerous without their primarchs that she tried to destroy them all.'

Malcador looked at him seriously. 'What are you saying, Constantin?'

'That if the primogenitors were truly scattered, can it be wisdom for us to seek them out? Should they not be left where they are? Destroyed? If they live, they will have the touch of their captors on them.'

Malcador nodded. 'A risk. But we did not get where we are now without taking risks.' He reached out and clapped Valdor's arm. 'We shall speak of this again. You shall speak of this with Him too, when He returns. Hone your arguments – I judge that He is determined to hunt for them. He has taken to referring to them as His "sons". Can you imagine that? Neither could I, until I heard it from His own lips. There might even be some lingering attachment, there, though how long it will last I cannot say.'

Valdor hesitated. 'Then His human sentiments – they are still ebbing.'

'As He predicted. All things have their price.'

At that, Valdor remembered what Kandawire had said, huddled against the cold as her dreams were dashed from her.

You let these things run loose now, you will not be able to rein them in later.

'Every step, in every direction, is hedged with danger,' Valdor said, darkly.

Malcador looked amused again. 'That has always been the

promise. Do not tell me you regret it, or I might begin to doubt your commitment to the cause.'

If he had expected Valdor to be angered by that, he was disappointed. The captain-general merely turned away, sweeping his long cloak about him and walking back along the gallery, leaving the Sigillite behind him in the shadows.

'How could you doubt that?' he said, speaking as if to no one in particular, or perhaps to someone who was no longer present. 'The cause is literally all I have. I can only hope, if we set out on this new course now, that we can say the same for these... sons.'

After an indeterminate period of induced coma, Samonas woke again into a world of excruciation.

Once conscious, it took him some time to recover his senses. At first, there was only the agony, flaring down every nerve and making his skin feel ripped up with hooks. After a while, he managed to control that using the techniques taught by the Order, and his surroundings settled into a blurred mask of just-tolerable pain.

He was in a medicae unit within the Tower, one he recognised from previous periods of post-battle convalescence. The walls were scrubbed clean and unadorned. Apothecarion drones clicked and whirred, running burbling fluids through their boxy innards. A few Tower menials busied themselves in the background, measuring samples and preparing solutions. Samonas watched them work, his eyes half-lidded, his battered body static on the metal cot.

That was all he was capable of doing for a long time. And then, just as he felt some strength beginning to twitch again in his prone limbs, the menials disappeared. The drones withdrew on their clattering rack-mounts, then shut down. The doors at the far end of the unit slid open, and his master entered.

Samonas summoned up his reserves, steeling himself for censure. As it was, the captain-general's bearing did not seem especially dark. If anything, he seemed more at ease than when they had last spoken in person.

'Recovering?' Valdor asked, coming to stand near the head of the cot.

Samonas couldn't move his neck yet, but managed to swallow thickly. 'I believe so,' he said.

'The body, surely. It takes more than flame to end that. But the mind? The spirit?'

'Acceptable.'

'You were charged with defending the Senatorum.'

Samonas felt the cold sliver of guilt strike right at his heart. There was no getting away from it. 'Yes,' he said. 'The failure was mine.'

'No, not really.' Valdor let the flicker of a half-smile play across his austere features. 'You wished to act sooner. I countermanded that. No blame attaches to your actions. Your role was not, as you supposed, to prevent her from reaching the Dungeon. It was to prevent her destruction from going any further. You did this with exemplary efficiency. More than I expected, in truth – there were no living Exemplars remaining by the time the Palace sentinels entered the tunnels. And of course, I did not even expect you to reach the Dungeon in time to face her in person. That was impressive, though you will bear some scars as reward for your speed.'

Samonas listened with gathering confusion. 'Not to... but I... the repositories–'

'I will say no more on it. You will ask no further questions. All is as it should be.'

For a moment, Samonas wondered if this were a dream – some kind of wish-fulfilment delirium. But then, he no longer dreamed.

'As you command,' he said, weakly.

Valdor leaned closer, inspecting the wounds Samonas had taken. He nodded perfunctorily, apparently satisfied that they would heal. 'There is a certain value to such activities,' he said. 'The risks are real, yet the rewards are significant. Genuine threats cannot be simulated, though they may be contained. I believe this model should be extended. When you are recovered, I wish you to look into it further for me.'

Samonas found this hard to follow. 'Your pardon, lord,' he said, wincing as his jaw clicked. 'I am not sure I understand.'

'I spoke to the Sigillite,' Valdor said. 'He is of the belief that our enemies indulge in games. Indeed, it is his judgement that they are bound by such things, which is both a weakness and strength to them. If we are to guard against them, we must do likewise. Generate threats, respond to them. Place our minds in the situation of those who wish to do Him harm. Let them in close, accepting the risk in return for the knowledge we gain. The stronger we become here, the more they will wish to bring us low. They have infinite facility – we must work to match that.'

As Samonas' mind gradually clarified, he began to see where this was leading. 'War games,' he offered.

'Of a kind,' said Valdor. 'What did the Thunder Warriors used to say, when they were sparring? The contest to first blood. That is what we must aspire to, only with this Palace, this one body, as the prize.'

Samonas began to feel light-headed. He guessed there were powerful neurosuppressors still swimming through his system. 'It shall be done,' he said.

Valdor stood straight again. 'Recover swiftly. There is work to be done when you are capable of it.'

There was always work to be done.

'As you command,' he said again.

And then, incongruously, there could be no doubt – Valdor

actually smiled. It was not a smile of amusement, nor of scorn, but something like accomplishment, as if a winding road had finally brought its traveller to a long-promised destination.

'You seem to have an affinity for the Dungeon,' he said. 'The labour will be arduous, but the place will not be left as a haunt of Astarte's old meddling. The Emperor has a new purpose in mind for it, one that will make it, in time, the most secure location in the entire galaxy.'

He withdrew, and as he did so Samonas felt his fragile consciousness began to ebb again. The recovery would be difficult, he could feel already.

'The Imperium is born, the Palace is secured,' Valdor said. 'All it needs now, I believe, is a Throne.'

EPILOGUE

It had to be off-world. The way things were going, there would be no corner of Terra free of scrutinising eyes soon. It was like a claw-grip, gradually tightening, gradually closing off the remaining light.

From the Palace she had gone quickly, making use of the skimmer taken from Kandawire's vehicle pool. In all the confusion, it had been surprisingly easy to slip into the night and keep going. By the time everything had calmed down and security started to get ramped up, she was a long way away and still running.

It had taken her only a few days to realise what she had to do. Off-world travel was rare and difficult to arrange, limited in theory to the Solar System sub-light network and the few intact mid-range routes beyond. After that, no one really knew how far it was possible to go, or what would be waiting for them if they got there. It was the great undiscovered vista left, now that the terrestrial field of imagination had been closed off so completely.

It had taken a lot of coin and a lot of careful perseverance, but in the end she'd found herself in the hold of a swollen-bellied hauler on the apron of a shabby orbital port in the nominally free republic of Haradh-Nu. Everyone on board was nervous – it was clear that this trip was not entirely legitimate, even by the standards of such legal hinterlands – and they behaved as if Imperial enforcers would come crashing on board at any moment to demand idents.

So she sat quietly by herself, her belongings heaped around her knees, checking the restraint-straps a hundred times and waiting for the countdown to begin. She knew the drill, in theory, but the practice still made her nervous. There would be a much bigger ship in orbit, she had been told. A starfaring vessel, one that had plied its trade even in the darkest of anarchy-ridden days and had overcome the worst the galaxy had to throw at it. Its captain was a man called, ridiculously, Alphoise de Ketasta-Phoel, who described himself as a 'rogue trader', which sounded absurd to her. Virtually everyone operating non-military starships worked outside the grasp of the Adeptus Terra, though that would surely change in the near future, and traders of any kind would not be allowed to be rogue for much longer.

She waited, sweating a little, feeling the deck heat up as the engines cycled to launch velocity. She was almost certain that a well-built ship would not allow its decks to get hotter like that, but she was committed now.

When the first boom hit, she started, clutching her armrests until her knuckles went white. A huge, crushing sense of inertia seized her, followed by a nauseating lurch into extreme speed. She saw the viewports raging with fire, and her seat shook wildly. That lasted for far longer than she wished for, and her stomach knotted painfully.

Then, finally, the worst of it subsided, and the viewport

cleared of its flames. She looked up again, still holding on tight, to see the starfield emerge and the grey-blue orb of Terra fall away. In the distance, she could already see the colossal hull of the *Arquebus*, hanging like an iron citadel in space.

It would take them over an hour to reach it. And after that, it might take days before they attempted to clear orbit and make for the void. Everything beyond that was uncertain, but there was a little time beforehand to take stock, to reflect on what she was doing.

As the worst of the shakes subsided, she unclipped her arm-restraints and reached for the device Kandawire had given her. It was still safe, still intact, though in all the long months of travel she had never dared access it. Now that she was out of Imperial control, even if only according to the letter of the law, it felt right to at least understand a little more. Her life was at risk, after all.

She clipped the audex-feed to her internal comm-bead and activated a security field around the augmitter. Then she sat back, made herself comfortable and started the transcript rolling.

In the void beyond, the rogue trader's galleon drew slowly closer.

'*Maulland Sen*,' came a voice Armina had never heard before – sonorous, confident, articulate. '*That is not a name I recall with any fondness.*'

She kept listening.

For her part, Kandawire had headed across the high plateau for many days, quickly running low on the few supplies she'd managed to find and beginning to doubt she'd survive to see the lowlands. As it turned out, the world beyond the Palace borders was kinder than she'd hoped – she was taken in, offered food, even given places to stay by those who occupied the many urban settlements of the Himalazian massif.

But she couldn't linger. News of the abortive assault on the Palace filtered back along the transitways rapidly, and squads of Arbites enforcers began to make frequent patrols. Among the wider populace, shock gave way to a wary fear – a sense that the bad old days weren't quite as far behind as everyone had come to hope.

So she kept moving, joining the crowds of itinerants who endlessly headed both to and from the beating heart of the Imperium – the traders, the generals, the chancers hoping to build a new life and the burned-out cases hoping to forget an old one.

No one recognised her. After a few days on the road, her environment suit became so battered that she might have been any old vagrant, and once the altitude got low enough for the climate to improve she discarded it for civilian clothing. She managed to access some of her old coin reserves from a semi-secure terminal in Ankandaa, which surprised her. Valdor could have had all that shut down, if he'd wanted to, and so clearly he hadn't intended her to starve.

After that, things got a little easier. She was able to hire a transport, and headed south-west across the boiling plains. As she did so, she remembered the trip to Ararat, its discomfort and its promise, and felt a prick of resentment. That already felt like a long time ago, in a world she had briefly been party to but was now banished from forever. The shaky flyers she had once taken for the sake of secrecy had been replaced by even shakier land-transports, and it was hard not to feel the force of the demotion.

The days turned to weeks. The Imperium was continually tightening security, it seemed, and so passage-warrants between provinces became harder to get hold of. The last big test for her – the short salt pan crossing to Zanbar on the eastern ridge-coast of Afrik – was particularly troublesome, and she had to expend the greater part of her dwindling coin stash in order to avoid serious trouble.

Once on the home continent again, though, she could relax a little. The smells of the old red earth, the dust in the air and the taste of charcoal from domestic burning took her right back. Everywhere she went there were signs of reconstruction and rebuilding, with whitewashed rockcrete cities rising up from the ashes of their despoiled forerunners. The Raptor Imperialis was flown proudly in these places, hanging listless in the hot, dry air but ready to flap wildly when the pre-rain wind boiled up out of the north.

It even began to feel good, to be stripped of all the baggage of responsibility. She had no influence, no power, not much money and just the clothes she wore, and yet there was a strange kind of freedom there, like a weight lifted after a long time locked in place.

She arrived back on a hot, humid night. The air was ripe with salt, and a stiff breeze was blowing from the east. Seeing the old places again after so long made her heart ache. No reconstruction had come here yet, and the ruins were more or less as they had been where the zooipa had left them, still black-edged and roofless. She walked down the old central street of the township, the dust clinging to her boots, and took in what remained of her childhood.

No one was left, not even the scavengers. A few hunchbacked dogs slunked in the dusk-shadows, whining weakly, but they loped off when she brandished a stick at them. By the time she reached the compound, out on the edge of town under the shade of a clutch of gnarled marula trees, the silence was almost unbearable.

She found her old room, open to the stars like everywhere else, and huddled into the corner. It even smelled somewhat familiar, despite the tang of ashes and the dung of the wild animals who'd made it their den before her. When fatigue caught up with her at last, she lay on her back and looked up at the stars, vivid and profligate in a clear summer sky.

This is the just the start – already the ships are being built that will carry this army into the stars.

That encounter felt like a dream, something that hadn't really happened. This was where she had always been meant to be. Escaping had been a mistake – she should have remained with her father, told one another stories and rebuilt a life amid the dry soil.

And yet, when she awoke the following morning, she saw that very little remained to be salvaged. If she wished to stay, she would have to start from scratch. She knew nothing of farming, and had no idea where the nearest intact settlements were. For all she knew, the place remained lawless, which had its disadvantages as well as its advantages. She was not a fighter – that much had already been proved.

Nonetheless, she did what she could. She managed to repair and activate the old water-purifier attached to the well out on the western edge of the compound. The power-unit in the generator had been looted, but she did find some tinned food in one of the old servants' quarters, hidden under a mattress and wrapped in straw. She gathered kindling from the bush outside and dragged it back, lighting a fire that she intended to keep burning the whole time. You had to keep the wild dogs away somehow.

It turned out that you could make a life here, if you were determined. Trader-caravans passed through from time to time, and she managed to find a few items of value that could be traded for seeds, fertiliser, dry goods, even a few out-of-date nutri-strips from Army supply depots. Still, she didn't expect to last long. It would be winter in just a few months, and when the rains came the lack of a roof would no doubt prove troublesome. She spent most of her time sitting on the old veranda, the wood rotting under her feet, watching the big orange sun slide into the west while birds called to one another over the darkening bush.

It was on one such evening, many weeks later, that she saw a man walking down the path towards the compound. His limbs looked out of proportion to his body, making his robes cling to him awkwardly.

She waited for him to reach her, saying nothing. When he sat beside her on the veranda's only other chair, she thought he looked horribly old. Had he always looked that old?

'You haven't done much with the place, kondedwa,' Ophar said, stretching his long legs out.

'Haven't had the help,' Kandawire said.

'Ah, it took me a while,' he admitted, grinning. 'But I got out, just like you told me. Now I'm here.'

Kandawire smiled. No doubt she'd hear the story in time, told at length, much of it embellished. 'I'm glad to see you.'

'I'm glad to see you, too.'

They sat in silence for a while. As the western horizon turned slowly golden, Kandawire sighed. 'I really messed it up, didn't I?' she said.

'You were right about most things,' Ophar said, shrugging. 'There are soldiers everywhere now. Doesn't matter who commands them – no one's pretending that this regime is different any more.'

She thought on that. 'Perhaps it was always futile, though,' she said. 'I could have kept my head down.'

Ophar chuckled. 'You're short enough already.'

Kandawire took a swig from her drink – a metal can with salty processed water in it – before handing it to Ophar.

'He wanted to talk,' she said at length. 'That's what I can't understand. He was ahead of us all the time, knew everything we were doing, and he still wanted to talk. He really didn't need to do that.'

'He was probably lonely.'

'I don't think they get lonely.'

'They're the loneliest people on the planet.'

Kandawire thought on that. Then she reached for her drink again. 'Planning to stay awhile?' she asked.

'I saw those fields you planted. Everything in them is going to die.'

She laughed. 'Oh.'

The sun began to sink, rippling in the evening heat.

'I was a High Lord, once,' she said, ruefully.

'And before that, you were mistress of this place,' Ophar said, not unkindly. 'You can be again.'

'I just don't want it all to be for nothing.'

'That's not for you to decide.'

'I guess not.'

Birds called out in chorus, crying eerily against the coming dark.

'We'll start building a roof in the morning, then,' she said.

'Just as you wish,' said Ophar.

ABOUT THE AUTHOR

Chris Wraight is the author of the Horus Heresy novels *Warhawk*, *Scars* and *The Path of Heaven*, the Primarchs novels *Leman Russ: The Great Wolf* and *Jaghatai Khan: Warhawk of Chogoris*, the novellas *Brotherhood of the Storm*, *Wolf King* and *Valdor: Birth of the Imperium*, and the audio drama *The Sigillite*. For Warhammer 40,000 he has written the Space Wolves books *Blood of Asaheim*, *Stormcaller* and *The Helwinter Gate*, as well as the Vaults of Terra trilogy, *The Lords of Silence* and many more. Additionally, he has many Warhammer novels to his name, and the Warhammer Crime novel *Bloodlines*. Chris lives and works in Bradford-on-Avon, in south-west England.

YOUR
NEXT READ

HORUS RISING
by Dan Abnett

After thousands of years of expansion and conquest, the human Imperium is at its height. His dream for humanity accomplished, the Emperor hands over the reins of power to his Warmaster, Horus, and heads back to Terra.

An extract from
Horus Rising
by Dan Abnett

'I was there,' he would say afterwards, until afterwards became a time quite devoid of laughter. 'I was there, the day Horus slew the Emperor.' It was a delicious conceit, and his comrades would chuckle at the sheer treason of it.

The story was a good one. Torgaddon would usually be the one to cajole him into telling it, for Torgaddon was the joker, a man of mighty laughter and idiot tricks. And Loken would tell it again, a tale rehearsed through so many retellings, it almost told itself.

Loken was always careful to make sure his audience properly understood the irony in his story. It was likely that he felt some shame about his complicity in the matter itself, for it was a case of blood spilled from misunderstanding. There was a great tragedy implicit in the tale of the Emperor's murder, a tragedy that Loken always wanted his listeners to appreciate. But the death of Sejanus was usually all that fixed their attentions.

That, and the punchline.

It had been, as far as the warp-dilated horologs could attest, the two hundred and third year of the Great Crusade. Loken always set his story in its proper time and place. The commander had been Warmaster for about a year, since the triumphant conclusion of the Ullanor campaign, and he was anxious to prove his new-found status, particularly in the eyes of his brothers.

Warmaster. Such a title. The fit was still new and unnatural, not yet worn in.

It was a strange time to be abroad amongst stars. They had been doing what they had been doing for two centuries, but now it felt unfamiliar. It was a start of things. And an ending too.

The ships of the 63rd Expedition came upon the Imperium by chance. A sudden etheric storm, later declared providential by Maloghurst, forced a route alteration, and they translated into the edges of a system comprising nine worlds.

Nine worlds, circling a yellow sun.

Detecting the shoal of rugged expedition warships on station at the out-system edges, the Emperor first demanded to know their occupation and agenda. Then he painstakingly corrected what he saw as the multifarious errors in their response.

Then he demanded fealty.

He was, he explained, the Emperor of Mankind. He had stoically shepherded his people through the miserable epoch of warp storms, through the Age of Strife, staunchly maintaining the rule and law of man. This had been expected of him, he declared. He had kept the flame of human culture alight through the aching isolation of Old Night. He had sustained this precious, vital fragment, and kept it intact, until such time as the scattered diaspora of humanity re-established contact. He rejoiced that such a time was now at hand. His soul leapt to see the orphan ships returning to the heart of the Imperium. Everything was ready and waiting. Everything had been preserved. The orphans would be embraced to his bosom, and then the Great Scheme of rebuilding would begin, and the Imperium of Mankind would stretch itself out again across the stars, as was its birthright.

As soon as they showed him proper fealty. As Emperor. Of mankind.

The commander, quite entertained by all accounts, sent Hastur Sejanus to meet with the Emperor and deliver greeting.

Sejanus was the commander's favourite. Not as proud or irascible as Abaddon, nor as ruthless as Sedirae, nor even as solid and venerable as Iacton Qruze, Sejanus was the perfect captain, tempered evenly in all respects. A warrior and a diplomat in equal measure, Sejanus's martial record, second only to Abaddon's, was easily forgotten when in company with the man himself. A beautiful man, Loken would say, building his tale, a beautiful man adored by all. 'No finer figure in Mark IV plate than Hastur Sejanus. That he is remembered, and his deeds celebrated, even here amongst us, speaks of Sejanus's qualities. The noblest hero of the Great Crusade.' That was how Loken would describe him to the eager listeners. 'In future times, he will be recalled with such fondness that men will name their sons after him.'

Sejanus, with a squad of his finest warriors from the Fourth Company, travelled in-system in a gilded barge, and was received for audience by the Emperor at his palace on the third planet.

And killed.

Murdered. Hacked down on the onyx floor of the palace even as he stood before the Emperor's golden throne. Sejanus and his glory squad – Dymos, Malsandar, Gorthoi and the rest – all slaughtered by the Emperor's elite guard, the so-called Invisibles.

Apparently, Sejanus had not offered the correct fealty. Indelicately, he had suggested there might actually be *another* Emperor.

The commander's grief was absolute. He had loved Sejanus like a son. They had warred side by side to affect compliance on a hundred worlds. But the commander, always sanguine and wise in such matters, told his signal men to offer the Emperor another chance. The commander detested resorting to war, and always sought alternative paths away from violence, where such were workable. This was a mistake, he reasoned, a terrible, terrible mistake. Peace could be salvaged. This 'Emperor' could be made to understand.

It was about then, Loken liked to add, that a suggestion of quote marks began to appear around the 'Emperor's' name.

It was determined that a second embassy would be despatched. Maloghurst volunteered at once. The commander agreed, but ordered the speartip forwards into assault range. The intent was clear: one hand extended open, in peace, the other held ready as a fist. If the second embassy failed, or was similarly met with violence, then the fist would already be in position to strike. That sombre day, Loken said, the honour of the speartip had fallen, by the customary drawing of lots, to the strengths of Abaddon, Torgaddon, 'Little Horus' Aximand. And Loken himself.

At the order, battle musters began. The ships of the speartip slipped forward, running under obscurement. On board, Stormbirds were hauled onto their launch carriages. Weapons were issued and certified. Oaths of moment were sworn and witnessed. Armour was machined into place around the anointed bodies of the chosen.

In silence, tensed and ready to be unleashed, the speartip watched as the shuttle convoy bearing Maloghurst and his envoys arced down towards the third planet. Surface batteries smashed them out of the heavens. As the burning scads of debris from Maloghurst's flotilla billowed away into the atmosphere, the 'Emperor's' fleet elements rose up out of the oceans, out of the high cloud, out of the gravity wells of nearby moons. Six hundred warships, revealed and armed for war.

Abaddon broke obscurement and made a final, personal plea to the 'Emperor', beseeching him to see sense. The warships began to fire on Abaddon's speartip.

'My commander,' Abaddon relayed to the heart of the waiting fleet, 'there is no dealing here. This fool imposter will not listen.'

And the commander replied, 'Illuminate him, my son, but spare all you can. That order not withstanding, avenge the blood of my noble Sejanus. Decimate this "Emperor's" elite murderers, and bring the imposter to me.'

'And so,' Loken would sigh, 'we made war upon our brethren, so lost in ignorance.'

It was late evening, but the sky was saturated with light. The phototropic towers of the High City, built to turn and follow the sun with their windows during the day, shifted uneasily at the pulsating radiance in the heavens. Spectral shapes swam high in the upper atmosphere: ships engaging in a swirling mass, charting brief, nonsensical zodiacs with the beams of their battery weapons.

At ground level, around the wide, basalt platforms that formed the skirts of the palace, gunfire streamed through the air like horizontal rain, hosing coils of tracer fire that dipped and slithered heavily like snakes, die-straight zips of energy that vanished as fast as they appeared, and flurries of bolt shells like blizzarding hail. Downed Stormbirds, many of them crippled and burning, littered twenty square kilometres of the landscape.

Black, humanoid figures paced slowly in across the limits of the palace sprawl. They were shaped like armoured men, and they trudged like men, but they were giants, each one hundred and forty metres tall. The Mechanicum had deployed a half-dozen of its Titan war engines. Around the Titans' soot-black ankles, troops flooded forward in a breaking wave three kilometres wide.

The Luna Wolves surged like the surf of the wave, thousands of gleaming white figures bobbing and running forward across the skirt platforms, detonations bursting amongst them, lifting rippling fireballs and trees of dark brown smoke. Each blast juddered the ground with a gritty thump, and showered down dirt as an after-curse. Assault craft swept in over their heads, low, between the shambling frames of the wide-spaced Titans, fanning the slowly lifting smoke clouds into sudden, energetic vortices.

Every Astartes helmet was filled with vox-chatter: snapping voices, chopping back and forth, their tonal edges roughened by the transmission quality.

It was Loken's first taste of mass war since Ullanor. Tenth Company's first taste too. There had been skirmishes and scraps, but nothing testing. Loken was glad to see that his cohort hadn't grown rusty. The unapologetic regimen of live drills and punishing exercises he'd maintained had kept them whetted as sharp and serious as the terms of the oaths of moment they had taken just hours before.

Ullanor had been glorious; a hard, unstinting slog to dislodge and overthrow a bestial empire. The greenskin had been a pernicious and resilient foe, but they had broken his back and kicked over the embers of his revel fires. The commander had won the field through the employment of his favourite, practiced strategy: the speartip thrust to tear out the throat. Ignoring the greenskin masses, which had outnumbered the crusaders five to one, the commander had struck directly at the Overlord and his command coterie, leaving the enemy headless and without direction.

The same philosophy operated here. Tear out the throat and let the body spasm and die. Loken and his men, and the war engines that supported them, were the edge of the blade unsheathed for that purpose.